DEEP WATER

Shadows of Camelot Crossing

A Haunting in Stillwater
Book 2

LISA COURTAWAY

LISA COURTAWAY

DEEP WATER

SHADOWS OF CAMELOT CROSSING
A HAUNTING IN STILLWATER BOOK 2

ISBN: 978-1-7374222-3-5 (ebook)

ISBN: 978-1-7374222-2-8 (print)

Editing and Formatting by Two Birds Author Services

www.twobirdsauthorservices.com

Cover Design by Miblart

www.miblart.com

Dedicated to Jesse and Claire, and in loving memory of Audrey and Paloma.

Can ghosts be evocation
Visions of those not lost but gone astray
Lingering traces of deeds pure or base

There are skeletons in every closet
Even a good turn can embolden its bones
Compelling it to have its secrets laid bare

Hidden from light
Shrouded in souls
Ever present still

Wrongs to be righted
Scores to be settled
Fates to be tempted

Must all good deeds be punished
No penance can quiet the haunt
The conscious vestige of unrest

Chapter One

2011

UNKNOWN SENDER: *It's time. Meet me at 32nd and Range at midnight. Bring the money.*

Wren got his text in the late hours of January 31, 2011. Although she didn't know the phone number, she knew the sender had to be Victor. She finished downing her second glass of wine while she read and reread his message. In her heart, she knew she shouldn't be drinking, but the day had been particularly hard on her; a little Chardonnay wouldn't harm the baby. The warm buzz from the wine did nothing to calm the instant thrill that quickened her pulse. It was as if a spell was broken, jolting her from a numb repose to an enlivened state. Even the colors in her darkened room become more vivid in an instant. She was watching *As the World Turns.* Wren never tired of watching old episodes of the soap opera, over and over again. For Christmas, her parents had all her old VHS recordings of the show transferred to DVD. The tapes were so worn, they'd have given out eventually. Thankfully the shows were saved before that. The series had always been an escape for her, and she was crushed when, several months earlier, it went off the air. She had always believed her life could be as exciting and perfect as the lives of the citizens of Oakdale. Now her chance had finally arrived. There was no internal debate. This was what she'd been waiting for since she was young. So certain her new life would be all she wanted, she didn't mind leaving the new DVD collection behind.

Wren didn't take time to reply to the text, just hurriedly set about preparing for her long-awaited departure. Victor never gave any specifics about when or how they would start their new lives together. She hadn't had a conversation with him since she'd been fired from the clinic where they both worked. But she was always certain he had a plan, a plan that included her. Though doubts had been creeping in, now she felt sorry for ever allowing those thoughts to drag her down. She had been right all along—he was coming for her. There was no need to pack much. She would need to wear as many layers as she could to brave the weather. Everything else could stay. She'd have plenty of money and time to buy a new wardrobe in Mexico, or wherever Victor decided they would settle.

A winter storm had already dumped several inches of snow; the wind chill hovered just above zero. She never paid attention to weather forecasts and didn't believe this storm to be anything beyond the typical come-and-go winter blasts that blew through Oklahoma on occasion. It would be much quicker to make it to the meeting place on foot. Many of the streets that wound their way through Camelot Crossing ended in abrupt dead ends and No Trespassing signs. If she left by car, she risked running off the road or getting lost. The crude path through the woods led to the place where Victor awaited to begin their new life.

She dressed quietly and quickly, building layers that could keep her warm in the snow but could be removed once she reached the warmth of Victor's truck. Before putting her coat on, she hung her purse cross-body. A quick survey of her dimly lit room prompted her to add two items to her bag. She wedged her phone and the photo on her side table into the purse. She almost left her phone charger before she remembered it, unplugging and stuffing it inside the suitcase between the stacks of bills bundled in Ziploc bags. He wouldn't notice the missing money. It was only a few hundred dollars short. Her anger and mounting sense of betrayal compelled her to spend the money on Christmas gifts for her family. She deserved it after all he'd put her through. Her rage had softened as she wrapped the presents, and penitence pressed her to buy a gift for Victor. She had never given him the monogrammed sterling cuff links, but now was her chance. The small, cheerily wrapped package sat on top of her dresser. She tucked it safely inside her coat pocket.

When she finished packing, she checked the clock. A moment of apprehension forced her to pause and deliberate for a moment, thinking of all she was leaving behind. To quiet her mind, she made her bed. Her children bounded to the forefront of her thoughts. Iva and Marlow were thriving under the care of their grandparents and aunt. Maybe she could send for them when she and Victor put down roots. Maybe she would leave them be. They were likely better off here, in their hometown where so many cared for them. Victor made it abundantly clear he wasn't interested in raising other men's children. It was too much to think of right now. She needed to go.

She cracked open her bedroom door and listened. One eye peered through the small opening down the stairs to the second-floor hallway, looking for motion, signs that someone was awake. *All clear.* Without further thought, she exited her attic room, closed the door behind her, and descended two flights of stairs, quietly, carefully avoiding the familiar squeaky boards that might give her departure away. When she was a teenager, she was a master at sneaking out. Now, she followed the familiar tiptoe path she had used all those years ago, amazed she remembered it still.

Through the kitchen window, she saw the blustery storm outside. This was more than the average squall she believed it to be. She wasn't dressed for a blizzard. She set her suitcase down by the door and went in search of more layers of winter clothing. In the laundry room closet, she found her dad's thick, winter coveralls and balaclava and donned the gear, which fit easily over all she had bundled up in. She returned to the kitchen, where she left through the back door—the closest exit to the rendezvous spot Victor directed her to in his text.

She froze as the door announced it had been breached: the familiar three beeps, followed by the pleasant voice, "Kitchen door open." The recently installed sensors gave her parents peace of mind that one of the kids could not slip outside and into the pool without notice. Her eyes darted to the ceiling, and she hesitated only for a moment, listening for footfalls or motion above. Hearing nothing, she proceeded on her mission.

Wind blasted her face, but the trapper hat protected her from the pelting snow. She pulled the door closed, unable to lock it from the outside; shielded her eyes from the punishing icy precipitation; and got her bearings. As she crossed the expansive wrap-around porch and stepped into the deepening snow, she didn't look back but plunged headlong across the back of the property, guided by rote familiarity to the trail that led through the Clarkson property to the cedar forest and the neglected dirt road beyond. The heavy downfall instantly erased any evidence of her passage. She knew this route well— all the dips and crevices, the caverns that jutted out from the wild terrain. The reality that she hadn't trekked through the woods in many years, and that the landscape might have changed dramatically since, never entered her mind. It would be more arduous to make it to her final destination through the relentless storm, but thoughts of her dream life propelled her forward. She wished she had checked the clock when she left but shook the notion from her mind.

Victor would wait for her.

As she made her way slowly through the freezing drifts, she tried to ignore the numbness in her feet and hands and focus instead on what turn of events may have led him to decide this was the night for them to leave Stillwater. He had been avoiding her for months. Even when she followed him into a store to feign a happenstance run-in, he looked right through her, never acknowledging their connection. She hadn't told him about the baby—hadn't told anyone. She dreamed of the moment when she could share the news with him.

Her arms burned despite the cold. Her muscles ached from the weight of the suitcase, which seemed to grow heavier with each step she took. The searing pain forced her to switch the case awkwardly from one hand to another. A pulsing heat built inside her, and she considered removing her dad's coveralls. Somehow, despite the warmth she felt, she was shivering. As her core temperature rose from the effort of navigating the ever-shifting landscape, she realized she had overestimated the articles of clothing she would need. A rivulet of biting sweat snaked down her neck. She stopped and set the suitcase down, turning her back to the wind to unzip the heavy garment. Her numb hands made the task difficult, and she struggled to get her fingers to securely grip the suitcase handle after she managed to lower the thermal overalls. She trudged on, unaware her course had shifted. No longer was she headed toward the intersection where her future waited for her in the comfort of an idling truck. Instead, she pressed on in the wrong direction, diverting further off track.

Then she heard his voice; at least she thought she did. He was yelling her name in perfect pitch with the howling winds. She spun around, searching for him, grateful he had come out to help her through the storm. And then she saw him. Although the figure was difficult to make out through the swirling snow, she was sure it was him. No one else would be in these woods at this hour, in this punishing storm.

Energized by his presence, she pushed forward. But her foot got stuck in a gnarled tree root, and she tumbled down a sharp incline, striking her leg on a fallen tree. She cried out in pain as sweat dripped into her eyes, mixing with the watery tears brought on by the wind and cold, blurring her vision. Thoughts skipped and slid away from her before she could process them. Confusion clouded her judgment. Her mind grappled with reality, but still she did not realize how lost she was. From the bottom of the ravine, she tried to come up with a new plan, but her mind wouldn't allow coherent thought to take shape. Hopefully Victor would be able to find her down here.

She was so warm. Her hand groped, unfeeling, along the icy walls of the gully when she fell forward into a hollow. She scrambled under the outcropping, seeking shelter, so she could clear her head and regroup. She clamored back as far as the small cavity allowed and pulled the suitcase in front of her, blocking some of the frigid gales. Intense blackness enveloped her; and for once in her life, she wasn't afraid of the dark. It was comforting almost, as if nature itself welcomed her in a strong embrace. Again she heard Victor's voice calling her. He was getting closer.

"I'm here, Victor," she yelled.

The cold seized her throat, choking out her voice, making it nothing more than a whispering croak. Her deflated plea couldn't penetrate the furious winds. She could wait here, sheltering from the unmerciful elements, until he made it down the slope. While she tried to come up with a plan, her mind struggled with wisps of lucid notions that escaped her before fully forming. She began to search her layers, seeking her phone. She could call him and direct him to her or flash a light to get his attention.

But it was no use. The idea was muffled and over-taken by a desire to calculate how far she had traveled, how much further she needed to go. These reasonings quickly evaporated, replaced by the need and struggle to remove her coat. She managed to free one arm from the oppressive clothing before her breathing eased, and she grew tired. A clear voice in her muddled mind told her to rest for a few minutes. Her final thoughts were that she just needed to rest. Consciousness left her before a massive tree was felled by the weight of the snow. Its expansive roots blocked the opening of the small cave; barring anything from entering or exiting.

Chapter Two

"Did you hear that?" Lula gasped, as she gripped her husband's arm with one hand and groped for her glasses on the bed side table with the other. She had to shake Roy a second time and then a third to stir him from his sleep.

"Roy, wake up. I swear I heard the kitchen door chime," she hissed, listening for another sound that might confirm her suspicion. All she heard was the whistling winds that pervaded the cracks around the windows and doors, and the ghostly howl from the chimney flues.

"You're dreaming, dear. No one would be out in this storm. Go back to sleep," Roy replied, attempting to keep the annoyance out of his tone and not rile his wife any further. If she got into a fuss, he might not be able to close his eyes for the rest of the night. He did his best to ignore the pulsing discomfort in his bladder while he drifted back to sleep.

Oklahoma's meteorologists had been right on the money when they forecast the freakish winter storm. If anything, they underestimated the snowfall and frigid temperatures that swept over Stillwater, Oklahoma, as January gave way to February 2011. It was rightly a blizzard, and it forced the entire state to stand still, holding its breath, until the snow stopped falling, the winds died down, and the bitter temperatures rose enough for folks to dig out from feet, not inches, of heavy white powder.

It was the night Roy and Lula Clarkson's youngest daughter made her escape, leaving behind two young children. In effect, they were left orphaned, as neither ever knew their fathers.

Lula tossed and turned the remainder of those cold, dark hours. She was bothered more by a nagging feeling that something wasn't right than by her husband's reverberant snores. Roy's choppy, snuffling breaths competed with the intemperate wails of the storm raging outside. Over twenty inches of snow fell, pelting the windows as it was tossed about madly in the high winds. For all of her sixty-eight years, Lula had lived in Stillwater. And she couldn't remember a time when winter had arrived so fiercely.

She gave up on sleep around five in the morning; the sun had yet to rise. She stopped in the hallway to nudge the thermostat up a couple of degrees and pulled her chenille robe tighter around her neck as she made her way downstairs, deftly side-stepping the creaking spots on each step so as to not wake her family.

As her slippered feet touched down on the last tread, she knew something was wrong. The icy chill she felt when she exited her bedroom, which she attributed to the plummeting temperatures outside, was unbearable on the lower level. Snow blew into the entryway from behind her. Puddles of slush lay against the carved wood baseboards in the hall at the foot of the stairs. Puzzled, she rushed to the kitchen, where the door stood ajar. Large drifts accumulated at the kitchen door, which was held open by the weight of the heavy powder, allowing more snow to fill the space. Visible plumes of vapor escaped through her lips as she kicked at the mound of snow, pushing enough out the door to clear the threshold. She pressed her tiny frame against the door with all her strength, fighting the wind. It took great effort, but she was able to close and lock the door. It must not have been latched tightly, leaving it vulnerable to the forty-mile-per-hour gusts. *She hadn't been hearing things last night*, she quietly mumbled to herself, cursing about how much heat had escaped and how her house slippers were likely ruined as she headed to the garage where she grabbed the seldom used snow shovel.

Back in the kitchen, she scooped as much of the melting mess as she could into a pile close to the door. She opened the door and was blasted by the violent winds and thrashing snow as she hurled the heavy mess outside. It was an impossible task, and she resorted to grabbing a stack of old towels kept in the laundry room, using them to absorb what they could. Her best bet would be to use the shop-vac, but she would wait until everyone was awake. The melting slush wouldn't harm the brick floors of the large house that was designed to look like a centuries-old Victorian farmhouse, even though it had been built little more than twenty-five years ago. She pushed the button on the Mr. Coffee before making her way back upstairs to change into dry clothes and get the last word in on the matter with Roy.

A snow day had been declared the night before, in advance of the anticipated storm. There was no need for Lula to rouse her grandchildren. They could get some extra sleep before they eagerly ventured out in the snow once the winds died down. The Clarkson property in Camelot Crossing sat atop one of the small hills that dotted the expansive neighborhood. Their acreage had been a popular sledding locale for the neighborhood kids since the snowfall in 1985 when the Clarksons first established roots in the stately development to the south of town. Lula knew it would be difficult to rein in her rambunctious grandchildren. It might not be safe to play outside in the white-out conditions but keeping them inside could prove impossible.

Despite the lingering chill in the dining room just off the kitchen, she took her coffee in her favorite spot in front of the picture window that framed the back of their property so beautifully, no matter what season. The fiery glow of a small space heater did its best to warm her feet while she cupped both hands around the mug of her hot brew. She could hear Roy moving about upstairs, readying himself for the day. She sipped her coffee and marveled at how differently this view had looked less than twenty-four hours earlier. The weather took her thoughts to indoor activities that might keep her grandchildren content. Maybe they would settle for baking cookies and roasting marshmallows at the fireplace.

She shook the ideas from her head, knowing they would insist on being outside playing in the most snow they had ever seen in their young lives. As she rose and made her way to the coffeepot for a refill, she heard small footfalls thumping on the floor above, followed by Iva and Marlow's heady laughter as they looked out their window and discovered the wintry wonder that had befallen their grandparents' property. Lula took a deep breath and a hefty swig of coffee and prepared herself for the whirlwind that was funneling down the stairs.

The lively twosome—Iva who recently turned five and her younger brother Marlow, almost four—jabbered excitedly about building snow forts and sledding.

"Do you have enough hot chocolate and marshmallows, Gram?" Iva asked. "Will Papa let us use his top hat for our snowman?" she continued, not pausing long enough for a reply. "I want Mommy to sled with us. Are you going to sled, Gram?"

Marlow stood by with an excited grin, eyes wide, nodding his head at his sister's eager inquiries, as Lula added brown sugar to the bowls of steaming oatmeal she had scooped from a pot on the stove.

"Yes, there's enough hot chocolate, but there aren't

enough marshmallows in the entire town for this blast. You know Papa won't let anyone use his top hat. Your mom might brave this cold but count me out. Now eat your oatmeal. It'll warm you up from within so you might last five minutes out there."

Amid all the excitement the winter squall brought about that morning, no one took notice that Wren—the youngest Clarkson daughter and mother of Iva and Marlow, usually an early riser—had not joined her children for breakfast. It wasn't until after the table had been cleared, when the children ran upstairs to wrap themselves in long johns, sweaters, and bibs, that Lula wondered why her daughter was still asleep.

Her grandchildren pressed against her as the three huddled in the confined alcove outside Wren's attic room. Both kids resembled patchwork starfish, bundled up in layer upon layer of clothing. Lula tapped gently on Wren's bedroom door. She could hear the murmur of the television on the other side. Unable to contain their excitement, Marlow turned the knob and the three fell forward, their momentum thrusting them into the room. It was dark. The curtains were drawn. The only light in the room glowed from the small television. Lula recognized the familiar faces of actors on Wren's favorite soap opera. She turned the TV off as Iva flipped on the light switch.

"Mommy, wake up! You have to come see—"

She stopped short as she saw the bed, empty and neatly made. Wren had never been one to make her bed.

The nightstand was vacant, void of Wren's phone charger and the cardboard picture frame adorned with glitter-painted macaroni that held a snapshot of the entire Clarkson family.

Iva ran down the stairs to the second floor, looking for her mom in the hall bathroom, but Wren was not there. Lula opened the closet; Wren's boots did not lay among the jumble of shoes on the floor. Her coat was gone, as was the antique suitcase that Wren had spent a lifetime covering with all manner of stickers. Its absence left a wide, empty gap on the closet's top shelf.

"Lula, where'd you hide my Carhartts and trapper hat?" Roy called from downstairs.

Chapter Three

Birdie Clarkson believed her younger sister was in bed with her when she woke in the early hours of that February morning after a restful sleep, her first in many nights. It seemed so real—Birdie felt wisps of her hair tickle her cheek, stirred by Wren's deep exhales. As Birdie came to, her mind clung to the notion that Wren was with her; the sensations so pervasive. The vision did not break apart and fade away like a normal nighttime dream. Despite the cocooned warmth provided by several layers of bedding, an icy shiver skittered down her spine. She sat up, pulling the heavy quilt with her, and drew back the curtain, taking in the view of Lowry Street where her small home sat. The quiet road near downtown Stillwater was lined with houses that were built in Stillwater's early years. The quaint homes were now blanketed in white.

Astonishment replaced the unsettling conviction that

she was not alone. The snow drifted halfway up the window. The white powder shone with a glowing aura as the morning sun struggled to penetrate the wall of flakes that fell from the heavy sky. At that moment, the hall light flickered, and she heard the quick beeping of the microwave before the house fell silent, void of the regular hum of appliances that are barely noticed until they are hushed.

Birdie stretched and let out an exaggerated yawn, recalling how the howling outside her window had distracted her from the nightly worrying, the anxiety that usually kept her wide-eyed until the dark hours of the morning. Wren's careless behavior was spiraling out of control again. Her parents were getting too old to take care of Iva and Marlow. The pressure had been mounting for Birdie to take action once more—get a bigger place, have the kids move in with her. Maybe Wren needed another inpatient stint to set her right one more time. Perhaps she would discuss the option with her parents, or she could simply take matters into her own hands. She abandoned those overwhelming notions, focused instead on the sounds of the raging storm outside, and slept well for a change.

Even while sleeping peacefully, she wasn't surprised Wren invaded her dreams. It made sense that she dreamed of Wren climbing into bed with her, as she had so often while growing up under their parents' roof. For someone as free-spirited as her sister, Wren also had unwavering behaviors, patterns that were predictable despite her complete abandonment of norms and rules. Insisting she sleep with Birdie during storms was a constant throughout the sisters' lives.

Birdie wasn't actually alone; her cat Cheshire stirred at the foot of the bed.

"There goes the power," she commented to her feline roommate.

Cheshire regarded her for a moment before rising, turning a full circle, and situating himself in the same spot he laid in all night.

"Never fear, Chesh, we'll stay warm. We've got loads of firewood and plenty of blankets."

The cat didn't acknowledge her words this time but accepted a head scratch before returning to his nap.

She tossed back the blankets, covering her cat, and slid her feet into her slippers. Being careful not to disturb the slumbering feline, she made the bed. A groan escaped her when she remembered that no power meant no coffee pot. Caffeine was a must if she was to get through the stack of math tests that needed grading. She went to the kitchen and rummaged through the pantry for a few minutes before conceding that she had no instant granules and would have to settle for green tea, grateful that she had never replaced the old, gas stove. Next, she poked around in the junk drawer before landing on a box of matches. It only took a second to light the pilot light. She put the kettle on and took a moment to warm her hands near the ringed blue flame.

In the tiny living room, she grabbed some fresh

kindling and several logs and set about starting a fire. The house was well stocked with firewood, thanks to her dad having chopped more than she believed she could possibly need. If the power wasn't restored soon, she'd make a good dent in the supply. Satisfied the fire would be roaring soon, she went to the window in the front room of her shotgun house. She had never seen so much snow in her life. As she turned to quiet the whistling kettle, she saw the reflection of her sister in the mirror over the fireplace mantle. A breathy gasp escaped her lips, but her sister didn't move. Her gaze darted to the other side of the room where Wren would be standing. There was no one there.

"I'm seeing things, Cheshire," she hollered to the cat. Apparently the burden of cleaning up yet another one of her sister's debacles weighed more heavily on her than she could admit. Oddly, the cat replied with a very dramatic yowl, which was surprising to hear from the typically indifferent feline. The large ball of fur scurried in front of her and settled into his fleece-lined cat bed in front of the fireplace.

"Chill out, little dude! You almost tripped me," she said, laughing as she noticed the raised ridge along the cat's spine and fluffed-out tail. "Guess you're seeing things too, Cheshire."

Her hands hugged the mug, and she leaned in close, warming her face on the steam that rose from the hot tea. She took the cup to the small dining room table where she took a seat and watched the snow fall on the deserted street outside. Her thoughts went to Iva and Marlow, as they often did. She wished she had accepted her parents' offer to ride out the storm in Camelot Crossing. The Clarkson property was even more beautiful when blanketed in white. Her excuse had been that she had too many papers to grade, and she couldn't be distracted. In reality, she hadn't anticipated the forecast to be so dead right and had no desire to listen to Wren drone on and on about how badly things were going for her. Her younger sister always had someone else on whom she could lay the blame for the challenges she faced. Wren never acknowledged her own role in the turmoil that followed her through life. Now Birdie was bummed she would miss the kids' excitement as they explored the wintry landscape of her parents' acreage.

The pleasant thoughts of the kids in the snow were snatched away in an instant as her mind turned to the dilemmas she faced. Mom and Dad had suggested Birdie start looking for a house that would accommodate the children. Since Wren had lost her job, she had been drinking and brooding and obsessing with a fervor she had never displayed before. Wren's behavior was putting the children's safety at risk, again. Iva and Marlow were becoming sullen. Iva couldn't focus on her lessons in kindergarten, and Marlow was lashing out in disobedience and even violence at preschool. Both kids' moods swung wildly with the instability. Birdie didn't think she could handle another round of the Wren-induced madness. Her sister would likely rebound just as Birdie upended her own life, moved to a new place, and got the kids established in a routine that would calm the chaos. As had happened before, Wren would simply expect Iva and Marlow to be handed back over to her, never giving thought to what the tumult would mean to her children and the rest of the Clarksons.

As her parents aged, Birdie could see the impact Wren's waywardness had on them. She took on yet another responsibility to spare Roy and Lula from the truth. She believed she could lessen her parents' humiliation and shame as Wren's actions became more sordid, criminal even. The things they knew already were enough to riddle them with guilt and self-blame. Birdie feared that the knowledge of their youngest daughter's true character might cause a heart attack, or worse. And so she vowed that they'd never know how bad things really were. The old *ignorance is bliss* adage drove Birdie's endeavors. She was their protector. She would stop at almost nothing to spare her parents the harsh truths of Wren's actions. Birdie needed to know Wren wouldn't put her, *them*, through that again. She was taking measures to make sure that didn't happen. Her sister needed a wake-up call, needed to be put to the test. Birdie doubted Wren's ability to rise to the occasion, and she dreaded the overwhelming steps that would need to be taken to set everyone on the right path.

Those thoughts were interrupted by her ringing phone. She'd left it on the charger on her nightstand down the hall. As she dashed to answer her phone before it went to voicemail, she caught another glimpse of something that didn't belong in the mirror above her dresser. She didn't register what she saw as she bent to grab the phone and slid the green bar.

"Hello," she gasped, wondering if she answered in time, noting it was her parent's home number.

"Birdie, your sister's gone," her mother belted out, not announcing herself.

Birdie turned to sit on her bed and noticed that it was a mess. The sheets and blankets she had smoothed and tucked this morning were twisted; one corner of the comforter hung off the side, almost touching the floor. The pillows were strewn about. Cheshire couldn't have done this. She caught the mirror image again. She forgot that her mom was on the phone as she stared. Behind her own reflection stood her sister. Wren was looking down at a bundle of pink blankets she held in her arm. She was swaying gently, as if comforting a baby. Wren's head snapped up, and she locked eyes with Birdie. Her face contorted into a silent scream. A dark labyrinth of veins could be seen through Wren's skin, which was an eerie blue. The whites of her eyes were red and angry. Birdie jumped and dropped the phone. Mirror Wren returned her gaze to what she held in her arms and began swaying again.

"Birdie, did you hear me? Are you there?" her mom's voice bayed from the phone. "I think I may have lost the call, Roy."

Birdie grabbed the phone and ran from her room,

tripping over a pair of shoes that lay outside her bedroom door. They were sandals that she hadn't worn nor removed from her closet in months.

"No, Mom, I'm here. What do you mean, Wren is gone?" As she paused in the hallway, her eyes darted to the bathroom doorway and into the living room beyond. She knew any direction she went she would be faced with a mirrored surface, so she remained in the hall, attempting to calm her nerves, slow her breath, lower her heart rate, and focus on the phone call.

"She's just gone. We woke up this morning and went to check on her. Her suitcase is missing, her phone—" Her mom trailed off.

Birdie could hear that her mom was pacing; her heavy breathing kept pace with her footfalls that echoed through the phone. She sounded frantic.

"Give me the phone, Lula. Go sit down; try to calm down," Birdie heard her dad say as there was a shuffling on the other end of the line.

"Hey, Birds, can you believe this snow?" her dad asked, sounding much more conversational than her mom.

"Yeah, it's crazy. I lost power about fifteen minutes ago. What's going on with Wren? How could she have left in this storm?"

"Well, you know your sister. She never lets practical matters stand in her way, always getting herself in over her head. My truck is still in the garage. She's been using it to get around since, well, you know. So she must've gotten a ride. Looks like she left through the kitchen door, which is odd. She left the dang door open; made quite a mess. The snow's been falling too fast to make out any footprints. Not sure what to make of it really. Hate to call the authorities; she'll come back soon, I'm sure. I'm expecting a call any minute now telling me she's with a friend, stuck in a drift somewhere and needs a tow. Try telling that to your mom, though. She wants to file a missing person report already." Dad's tone spoke to his complacency. Yes, it was foolish for Wren to take off in this weather; but no, it wasn't inconceivable.

"You're probably right, Dad," Birdie replied, leaning against the wall. She was beginning to calm, the conversation distracting her from the tousled bed, spooked cat, and errant shoes in the doorway. "I wouldn't bother the authorities with something like this. I'm sure their hands are full with real emergencies right now."

"That's what I told your mother. I suggested she give you a call and see if you had heard from her."

"No, not a word, but she usually doesn't alert me to her whims," Birdie replied. Her thoughts drew away from the call, shifting from concerns about Wren to fears about herself. She was already forming her own denial of what she had seen in the mirror; her mind mulling over rationalizations for the frightening anomalies that rattled her so.

"Well, if you hear from her, let us know. You going to be okay without electricity? It's still on out here."

"Yeah, I've got plenty of firewood thanks to you, and

I can light the pilot light on the stove. The thing is so old it doesn't have an electric ignition. If it goes on too long, I can put my fridge stuff in the garage. Pretty sure it's cold enough out there to keep it from spoiling. I'll grade as many papers as I can in the daylight and curl up with a flashlight and a book later on. I should be able to ride this out for several days just fine. Cheshire and I can sleep by the fireplace if need be."

"Well, that's good. I'm gonna go, hon. Try to calm your mother down. The kids are a little thrown off by their mom's absence but are more interested in building a snowman at the moment. Take care!"

"Will do, Dad. Keep me posted."

Birdie ended the call but remained in the hallway. She was spooked by seeing her sister in the mirror but chalked it up to her own conscience—a guilty mind fabricating things that weren't there. Stress-induced visions. Wren made her own decisions. Birdie had nothing to feel guilty about. Who knew where Iva and Marlow would be today if Wren didn't have Birdie and their grandparents? It was just like her sister to take off, even if it was during Snowmageddon.

Having talked herself down from her shock and fear at her presumed hallucinations, she entered her bedroom again. She kept her eyes cast down, not chancing another look in the mirror, and took her copy of *The Shining* from her nightstand. She flipped the book upside down and put it in the bottom drawer, then laughed at herself for thinking it would be a good reread during the winter storm. It would be easy to find something else to read later. Next she straightened her bed, telling herself she must have skipped making it after being surprised by the power outage. As she kicked the misplaced shoes under her dresser, she surmised that Cheshire must have dragged them out from somewhere and left them in the doorway—the staunchly indoor cat's version of bringing its kill to its owner.

The mountain of papers piled on her desk mocked her, so she went back to the kitchen, topped off her cup of tea, and retreated to her office to get to work. Settling in, she heard a voice in the next room and went to investigate. The television had come on, which meant the power was back on. She took no note of the program that played out on the TV as she went to the light switch, flipping it up and down to no avail. She went to the kitchen and saw that the clock on the microwave wasn't flashing 12:00 as it would if the power were restored. The lights refused to come on in the kitchen as well.

Passing back through the living room, heading towards the garage to check the breaker box, she now saw the program on TV. It was an old soap opera, *As the World Turns*. She didn't think the show was still on the air, but it had always been Wren's favorite. Her sister had obsessively recorded hundreds of episodes and watched them over and over again. In an effort to reduce the stockpile of VHS tapes, her mom and dad had all the tapes converted to DVD. They gave the disk collection to Wren for Christmas. You would've thought they gave her keys to a brand-new car. Birdie had never understood her sister's obsession with the melodrama, but Wren insisted the DVD set was one of the best gifts she'd ever received. The episode on her television saw the citizens of Oakdale grappling with their own snowstorm.

There were no blown fuses, nor flipped breakers—no explanation of how only the television had regained power. None of it made sense to her, but she was no electrician. She walked back to the living room and used the remote to turn the TV off. As she did so, she kept her head lowered, allowing her hair to cover her eyes, not wanting to glimpse the mirror; then she went back to the tiny office and forced herself to focus on grading.

That night, the relentless winds had died down, but the snow continued to fall, and there was still no power. Birdie's back ached from the hours spent slumped over the papers she graded, and her eyes burned from attempting to decipher the handwriting of dozens of college students. She had diligently stoked the fire all day; log after log thrown onto the blaze to keep the chill from penetrating the darkened house. At nightfall, she gave up on the grading. In the kitchen, she rummaged through the drawers to find a manual can opener. While she waited for her soup and water to boil, she called her mother.

"Hey, Mom, any word from Wren?"

"Not a one. Thank goodness the kids wore themselves out, or they'd be asking questions. If she's not home by tomorrow, I don't know what I'll do. Her phone goes straight to voice mail. Who knows how many messages I've left for her." Lula's voice held a tinge of fear that bordered on panic.

"That's so Wren. Quit your worrying. She'll be back soon."

"Something seems different this time, Birdie," Lula said pensively.

"Relax, Mom. Hey, I'm trying to save the battery on my phone, so I need to go. Give the kids a hug from me and stop stressing. Good night, Mom. Love you." Birdie disconnected the call before her mother could reply.

Anger mounted in her as she ate her soup by candlelight. How dare Wren cause everyone to worry so! Birdie knew from a young age that her sister only cared about herself. That awareness caused her to wonder why she was ever surprised by Wren's antics.

Outside, all lay quiet; save for an occasional branch snapping and falling, finally losing its battle under the immense weight of the snow, or the wheels of a brave driver spinning helplessly as they tried to free their cars from the mountains of white powder. Just as Birdie tilted the soup bowl to her mouth, noise from the television forced out the silence. She jumped and spilled a trail of tomato soup down the front of her hoodie. Cursing under her breath, she blotted the red mess from her top and made her way to the television. She reached down and angrily yanked the plug from the outlet, wondering what kind of weird fluke could allow for power in one outlet amidst an otherwise complete blackout. A hush fell upon the house again.

She carried a candle through the hallway and into the bathroom. As she brushed her teeth, she kept her back turned to the mirror. In her bedroom, she dug out two extra comforters from the antique trunk at the foot of her bed. She remained fully clothed in thermals underneath the sweatpants and hoodie she'd worn all day. It was too cold to change clothes. As she situated herself under the pile of blankets, she made an exaggerated kissy-smacking sound with her lips and cooed, "Cheshire, come to bed. We can help keep each other warm." The cat did not appear.

Birdie rolled over, turning her back to the hallway door and giving up on her cat joining her. As she began to drift off, she felt the weight of the cat hopping onto the bed, and she awaited his pawing at the blankets. While waiting for Cheshire to settle in, she heard a familiar noise and felt a gentle stirring at her back. Although she hadn't heard the sound in years, outside of this morning's dream, she immediately recognized the soft snores of her younger sister.

Birdie bolted upright. The cat was not in the bed with her. A chill rushed over her that wasn't caused by the frigid temperature. She got up, snatched her pillow and several blankets off the bed, and went to the floor before the fireplace, where Cheshire was still curled up. The wood floor was warmed by the blaze, but she knew sleeping on the hard surface wouldn't be the most restful.

She tossed and turned for a bit, pushing thoughts of her sister out of her mind. The cat sensed his person had settled, so he joined her, pushing his way beneath the covers. To Birdie's surprise, she slept soundly through the night.

Although the electricity was still not on, she woke the next morning to sounds on the television. On the screen was a woman—despite the grainy black and white footage, Birdie could tell she was smartly dressed.

"Good morning, dear," the black and white woman said.

From her vantage point on the floor, Birdie could see the plug laying below the outlet. She crawled across the floor, untangling herself from the blankets as she went. She groped for the power button and was relieved that the screen went dark. She decided the television powering on by itself while plugged in was far less distressing that its coming on while unplugged, so she pushed the prongs back into the socket. As she rose, she saw her sister in the mirror above the fireplace. Wren ignored Birdie. Her attention was focused on the bundle in her arms.

Chapter Four

BEFORE

Tending to Wren's whims had been Birdie's burden from early on. It was no small task keeping the girl safe and out of trouble. Ever since she was a small child, Wren had always sought excitement. The way she would bound out the back door of their childhood home in pursuit of a herd of deer. She would heedlessly chase the animals into the forest, barefooted, without announcing her departure to anyone. When she returned home as the sunlight faded, her knees would be scraped, and her feet would be bloodied and caked in drying red mud.

"I wanted to see where they lived," she would explain with a casual shrug as she pulled brambles out of her tangled hair. It was Birdie who was scolded for not keeping a close enough eye on her younger sister.

Birdie learned to be in a state of constant alert whenever Wren was in her care. Wren would bolt from the sidewalk and into the street before the traffic light announced her right of way, wrenching free of Birdie's grasp to be the first on the bus. She climbed too high into trees and swam too far out at Lake McMurtry, always pushing the limits.

When the girls became teenagers, Wren's lust for exhilaration intensified. She always managed to worm her way into Birdie's weekend plans, even if it was just taking a spot in the backseat of Birdie's car while they cruised Boomer Lake. The lake's paths and picnic spots hosted family outings during the day. After dark, they became a traditional late-night hangout for Stillwater teens.

"Please let me go with Birdie to Boomer," she would whine to their father. "I'm so bored! I've done all my chores and homework. Please, Daddy!"

Wren never accepted the word *no*. Birdie wondered why her parents ever attempted to dissuade her younger sister from something she desired. Roy and Lula were too worn out by Wren's unending demands to put up much of a fight. So Wren would tag along for everything. Whether Birdie was cruising Boomer Lake on hot summer nights, going to the movies, or a high school dance, Wren always came along. Roy and Lula naively believed that Wren was responsible enough to be out on her own, in the presumed safekeeping of her older sister. The two girls were barely two years apart in age. Despite the insignificant age difference, Roy and Lula never questioned Birdie's prudence. She was the responsible daughter, the keeper, the one they could always rely on.

Wren always disappeared, tasking Birdie with tracking her down. At Boomer, Birdie would wander through the parked cars, feeling foolish as she interrupted young couples who were busy fogging car windows with their impassioned breath. Birdie usually found her younger sister sharing a cigarette with a boy she didn't recognize—a fraternity jock who Wren had lied to about her age or a dropout from Perkins or one of the other little towns that dotted the map around Stillwater. Often, when a group of friends saw Birdie approach, they would simply point a finger in the direction Wren was last seen going. Birdie, the chaperone, never had a chance to fully enjoy her social life. The Clarkson girls rarely made it home in time when Wren tagged along. It was always Birdie who took the heat for breaking curfew.

Wren was barely fourteen years old when she became a familiar face with the town's law. She'd been caught in the backseat of a souped-up Chevy, drag racing down the country roads past Lakeside Golf Course. Wren's face was still flushed, her eyes wild when she hopped into the backseat of their dad's station wagon that night.

"Woohoo, Birdie-Bird, you should've been there! It was a wild ride!" she exclaimed shamelessly, drumming on Birdie's headrest from the backseat as Dad shook the officer's hand before climbing into the driver's seat. He didn't speak a word the whole drive home from the police station.

Whether it was scaling the slippery walls of the old water tower in Camelot Crossing or lifting a rollerball of

Bubble Gum Kissing Potion from Abbey's Hallmark, or a cassette tape from Hastings, Wren always sought the spark of risk. It was as if she needed the jolt of adrenaline as much as the air she breathed. Wren had a penchant for getting herself into deep water, never once considering what it meant to those who were forced to rescue her over and over again.

When they were younger, Birdie admired her sister's aplomb, though she'd never admit it out loud. She marveled as Wren loitered outside Brown's Bottle Shop until she spotted the perfect patsy. Her sister would bat her eyes at a guy and convince him to buy her a six-pack. When her target returned with her loot, she'd pull the lining from the pockets of her cut-off shorts out with a shrug and "pay" the hapless sap with a lingering kiss on the cheek. Wren's pulse never quickened as she secreted the room-temperature beer past the ticket counter at the Satellite Twin. Birdie never sat in the same row as her sister but could hear the snap-fizz of a can top popping, followed by her sister's hushed giggles before the opening credits rolled. After the movie, Wren would wind her way through LeMan's Arcade with a slightly off-kilter gait, looking for her next mark, someone who could make her night more adventurous.

Birdie would never dare pull the stunts Wren did; and if she tried, she couldn't have pulled them off with Wren's near-perfect success rate. Of course, Wren could never have been so successful if Birdie weren't so willing to cover for her. Wren flashed her fake I.D., which she had secured in Tulsa before she turned sixteen, at the doors of some of the town's looser establishments, using her looks to quiet any doubt the doorman might have about her age or the authenticity of her identification card. Birdie was forced to linger near one of the bars on The Strip, waiting for her sister to emerge, hoping she would do so alone and not in the company of a boy, or worse yet, a bouncer. She never considered abandoning her sister in those situations. The thought of disappointing her parents was too much for her to bear. If she were honest with herself, the concern they would be more disappointed in her than in Wren was the overriding motivation that kept her there, wasting her night out, alone on the curb in front of a college dive bar. At times, Birdie was certain Wren might prefer to get caught. Being exposed would raise the stakes, and Wren was always looking to up the ante; to push further into deep water.

Contrasting and balancing Wren's lust for all things taboo required Birdie to keep her head down and follow the straight and narrow. "You're such a fuddy-duddy milquetoast, Birdie," Wren would goad any time Birdie tried to ease her younger sister into something more conventional, like staying at The Teen Center dances instead of sneaking out the back door; or remaining in the stands at Hamilton Field to watch the game, not ducking under the bleachers with a boy. Birdie knew her parents preferred her stick-in-the-mud ways over Wren's brash nature, but the proverbial squeaky wheel got all the grease. Birdie's accomplishments were constantly over-shadowed by her younger sister's misdeeds.

For the most part, Birdie didn't mind being eclipsed. When resentments did creep in, Birdie would push them aside and try to rise above the pettiness. She was smarter, kinder, and more level-headed than Wren—traits she believed would help her excel while Wren was destined to deteriorate. Her looks bound to fade; her poor decisions certain to do her in.

Her baby sister was made for the spotlight. Birdie was no ugly duckling, but her curly dark hair and gray eyes paled next to her sister's golden locks and bright eyes. Birdie dressed the part of the studious, responsible girl, while Wren saw clothing as another way to flaunt her spirited personality. Wren worked to shake things up in Birdie's life. She'd flop herself down on Birdie's neatly made bed, ruffling the pin-straight corners. "Life's too short to waste time making a bed, Birdie-Bird," she would tease.

Wren prodded to spice up Birdie's wardrobe, as well. She would untuck Birdie's Oxford shirts and suggest Birdie ditch her preppy boat shoes for something with more flair. "I left my Jellies outside your door. That outfit would look way better with them or Keds. You're in high school, Birdie, not a retirement home!"

As strong-willed, fearless, and carefree as Wren could be, she had her weaknesses. She was afraid of the dark and never slept with the lights off. The girl would leave her small television on at all times; the noise and the light compensating, casting loneliness aside and forcing shadows out of the corners. Wren hated storms as well, and Oklahoma weather could be tumultuous. When lightning lit up the night sky and the house shook with fierce thunderclaps, Wren would climb into bed with Birdie.

"The storm is too much, Birdie. Scoot over, make room for me," she would whisper.

Wren knew better than to turn the lights on in Birdie's room. But she never took care to slip into her older sister's bed quietly. Before Birdie could get comfortable enough to fall back asleep, Wren would be snoring, a subdued drone, one that was annoying enough to rob Birdie of an hour or more of sleep.

Wren had cost Birdie so much over the years. Birdie was accustomed to living in Wren's shadow, but as they got older things became more contentious between the two. Wren's penchant for thrill-seeking grew more costly for all the Clarksons, especially Birdie. She made it her mission to shield her parents from Wren's calamities. Unlike other siblings who might be apt to snitch on their brother or sister, Birdie would go to great lengths to spare Roy and Lula the details of Wren's foolishness. It was partly self-preservation, but mostly she covered for Wren because she couldn't stand to see the disappointment on Roy and Lula's faces.

Somehow, those closest to Wren were the ones to take the blame on for the troubles her own schemes brought about. Birdie carried the brunt of that burden, forging a bitter disconnect that only grew stronger as they grew older. But when Wren became a mother, the weight and consequences of her selfishness were forced onto her children's tiny shoulders. Again, Birdie rose to the challenge; and in doing so, lost all prospects of fulfilling her own life's dreams.

Chapter Five

Jacob Summers had been Birdie's world. Since the day they met as young, assistant professors at Oklahoma State University, the two had been devoted to each other. They shared so much in those fourteen years: a home, careers, a simple, steady love, and a bond built from understanding and heartache. When he left, she didn't know what her world would become. Aside from cleaning up the devastation left behind by Hurricane Wren, Birdie felt she had little purpose. She was chained to the never-ending strain of putting the pieces back together and mending the wounds caused by her sister's chaotic, narcissistic take on life. But when she had Jacob, she had hope. Hope that she could untangle herself from Wren's messes and focus her attention on her own pursuits. Jacob never made Birdie feel less than Wren. It was one of the reasons she loved him so. He was drawn to more than Birdie's straight-laced, quiet beauty; he loved her mind and her ardent ways.

Birdie said goodbye to Jacob in the Tulsa airport. He was leaving for his dream job—teaching English to students in The Netherlands. He wanted her to join him, but the way things were, Birdie couldn't fathom pulling it all off. She would have to learn to speak Dutch in order to find work in Holland, and she chided herself relentlessly for never paying heed to Jacob's attempts to draw her into the language. Its hacking plosives and gasping cadence were difficult for her; besides, she had always been a numbers person.

He took her heart with him, but she held no ill feelings toward him. It was her fault. Her inability to see past the tiny, helpless faces of her niece and nephew kept her from chasing her own dreams. They needed her, so she couldn't start a life with Jacob, far away from Stillwater, Oklahoma, in a place where she could live for herself. It wasn't in the cards.

"I know you have a lot to sort out here, Bird," he whispered in her ear as they embraced for what seemed like hours at the entrance to security. "When things settle, you'll join me."

Behind his neck, Birdie twirled the inexpensive engagement ring around her finger. It was an absentminded habit she had formed in the almost three years she'd worn the tiny diamond. Her tears left a growing wet spot on his collar. She nodded her head feebly, willing his words to be true. She would tend to Iva and Marlow while Wren recovered from her latest fiasco. And then she would leave this world behind. That was the hope, the dream that remained unfulfilled. He never asked her to return the ring, even after they both knew they would not be united as husband and wife.

Instead, she became everything to her young wards, and focused all her energy on giving them some semblance of normalcy. Drying the tears, answering unanswerable questions, chasing away the demons their mother brought into their world, and providing stability. None of those things mattered to her sister as she bounced in and out of rehab, as countless men entered and exited her life, and she lost job after job. Through the years, Birdie was always there to pick up the pieces and care for the children.

Roy and Lula didn't have the energy to keep up with the active kids, and they certainly didn't have the strength to set the boundaries that Iva and Marlow desperately needed. If they had been capable of imposing limits they would have done so for Wren, and perhaps everything would have turned out differently.

No one knew who the children's fathers were. There was little doubt each child had a different daddy. Neither had the wavy blond hair and crystal blue eyes of their mother. Iva had thick, curly auburn locks, while Marlow had smooth, shiny hair that was black as coal. None of the small family looked like they were related. Iva's green eyes filled with tears at the slightest injustice. Marlow's dark eyes became darker as he fought to keep a cool face.

The two couldn't be more different, nor could they be more loved by Birdie, not even if they had been her own. She could never grasp Wren's inability to value that bond and do right by her kids. And she always wondered if the men who put life into Wren's belly, first when she was thirty-five and again when she was barely thirty-six, even knew they had offspring. It was a wonder Wren hadn't become pregnant when she was younger. Perhaps she had and kept it from her family while she did away with any unwanted pregnancies. Children would be a burden she had no interest in carrying in her youth. Birdie almost believed that the children were something Wren could gloat about. Wren knew Birdie's desire to be a mother was strong. When Wren realized Birdie would never bear children, she saw her chance to prove there was something she could do that her older sister could not. Maybe Wren thought children could fill a void in her life; no one would ever know. Roy and Lula had given up on becoming grandparents and could not contain their excitement at the opportunity to do so, regardless of the timing. Both conceptions had undoubtedly occurred during flings at some rehab facility or state hospital, maybe a halfway house; any one of the unconventional places Wren had called home since she fell under the spell of drugs before she completed her first year of college.

It had been easy for Birdie to ignore Wren's transgressions before the children were born. Birdie flippantly listened as her parents rehashed her sister's misadventures. She sat in judgment that her sister was given the same ample opportunities for success that she herself had; but instead strayed so far. It pained Birdie to see her parents grapple with what went wrong, blaming themselves for Wren's destructive flights of fancy. They were too consumed by all that was wrong with Wren to celebrate all that was right with Birdie.

Before Wren announced her first pregnancy by showing up to a family brunch at Mom's Place with a growing bump in her midsection that she could no longer hide, Birdie had imagined her own wedding and baby showers. She could envision the pride beaming from her parents' faces as Roy gave Birdie away to Jacob, and when Lula held her first grandchild. Presented with Wren's surprise announcement, Roy and Lula's expressions gave off unconcealed concern. Roy nervously rearranged the silverware on the table and cleared his throat repeatedly as if pushing back words that fought to be said. Lula grabbed his hand before he could reposition the sugar spoon one more time, and gently squeezed his fingers to release her own pent-up trepidation. Their clasped hands tapped the table rhythmically, as Roy used his free hand to remove a handkerchief from his pocket and dab the space above his lip, below his nose. Birdie had seen this pantomime many times over the years, her parent's rote reactions to the uncertainties Wren lobbed at them. But it was impossible to miss the shadow of anticipation and excitement the elder Clarksons felt at the thought of a baby, regardless of the circumstances.

Under the table, Jacob rubbed Birdie's hand as she fought back stinging tears that threatened to spill over. She and Jacob were not yet married, of course, but recently suffered another miscarriage. Her doctor was surprised that she had actually conceived and warned her not to try again to avoid the pain of another loss. She had to face the reality that she had waited too long. Birdie blinked hard and put a smile on her face, a congratulatory lilt in her voice; despite the devastation she felt knowing her time was up. She would never be a mother.

Birdie seethed with anger and despair as her attempts to become a mother failed in one miscarriage after another, while Wren found herself with child effortlessly and in quick succession. She and Jacob attempted to become parents even before they got engaged; the running joke being that perhaps a pregnancy would nudge them down the aisle. Their hopes were dashed three times before they gave up on the effort without discussion, sharing an unspoken awareness that yet another dream of theirs would never come true. Part of Birdie believed this was one reason Jacob set his sights on a faraway country. He didn't have the heart to make a clean break. At times, she resented his long, drawn-out approach to letting her go.

Wren proved she wasn't up for the task of mother-hood from the get-go. Birdie and her parents were on high alert at all times in the months following Iva's birth. Not ready to be tied down, Wren made a habit of dropping the infant on anyone who had an empty arm or free day. It was then that Birdie began to view herself as the real mother of tiny Iva. While rocking the infant to sleep, she would close her eyes and imagine Iva had been born to her. Thankfully, Jacob was too consumed with his professional goals to put up much of a stink over the canceled date nights and mounting grocery bills.

Birdie and her parents had eased themselves into a comfortable routine, caring for Iva, when Wren exited another rehab facility with a rounder face, heavier breasts, and her belly swelling again. Things only got more challenging when Marlow was born; possibly battling the effects of something illicit his mother had forced upon him while he was in the womb, a couple of weeks premature, and plagued with a distemper that made him colicky and difficult to soothe.

The unlikely parental conjunction comprised of the flighty Wren, the busy Birdie, and the exhausted Clarkson elders, struggled to manage the two children. As difficult as it was, no one was prepared when Wren's penchant for higher highs almost ended her life. They all should have seen it coming. Wren's lifelong obsession with tragic artists, bad boys, and shady men; her moods; her issues; and even the poetic names she had given her children, spoke to a propensity for the overly dramatic. Wren was never content.

None of the Clarksons were aware of Wren's growing issues with Adderall. Her dependency on the medication prescribed by her doctor was easier to hide than her previous struggles with street drugs, and she'd hid it well. Her family had noticed a positive change in her. She seemed calmer, focused, more capable of responsibility. They assumed that Wren was finally settling down, easing herself into being the dutiful mother the Clarksons had wished she would be. So Birdie was surprised when her sister called her that day. Birdie was between classes and was planning on running some errands for Jacob as he prepared for his departure. Wren didn't bother with niceties; she jumped right to the meat of the call.

"Birdie, would you mind taking the kids off my hands for the weekend?"

The request seemed innocuous, and Birdie loved spending time with the children.

"I've been having a really hard time sleeping and it's getting to me," Wren pleaded unnecessarily.

"I'll come by after my last class and pick them up. Just pack a bag for each of them," Birdie replied, already envisioning sitting on the couch, reading books to Iva as she cradled Marlow.

"He just cries so much," said Wren. She sounded exhausted and on edge. In the background, Marlow's cries never ceased.

When Birdie arrived at Wren's apartment a couple of hours later, eager to start her weekend with the kids, she found Wren asleep on the couch. Iva was playing quietly with a doll, while Marlow wailed in his crib, unattended.

"Wren, wake up!" Birdie urged her sister.

Unable to evoke a response from Wren, Birdie ran to

Marlow's crib, which was wedged between the wall and the double bed in the single cramped bedroom that Wren shared with both her children. She scooped up the crying infant and tried to console him as she ran to the bathroom and grabbed a towel, running it under the tap and wringing it out with one hand. Her attempts to quiet the baby were pointless. Birdie wondered when he had last had a bottle or a diaper change. She almost knocked Iva over as she hurried back to her unconscious sister. The child had been following Birdie, watching in quiet confusion.

"Oh, Iva, I'm so sorry, sweetie. How long has Mommy been asleep?" As soon as she asked the question, she knew the young girl wouldn't have the answer.

"Mommy won't wake up," was all Iva replied.

Back in the living room, Birdie pressed the towel to her sister's face; stopping briefly to secure the fussy Marlow in his bouncy seat. Iva had become entranced by a soap opera on television. Birdie returned her attention to her sister who barely stirred. She called 9-1-1, and as the dispatcher asked what her emergency was, Iva turned to Birdie and said, "Mommy's missing her show."

The minutes spent awaiting an ambulance were some of the most terrifying of Birdie's life and seemed to last for hours. Not knowing what to do with that time, she prepared a bottle for Marlow and brought the bouncy seat close to the couch. She fed the child while watching Wren, paying close attention to the rising and falling of her chest. When help arrived, she took the children to the bedroom and settled a sleeping Marlow into his crib and turned cartoons on for Iva. Then she stood by numbly as paramedics tended to Wren.

"Do you know what she took?" a young EMT inquired.

She couldn't believe the medic's calm demeanor and struggled to process what he asked. The strobe effect of the flashing lights through the curtains was dizzying and cold sweat dripped down her face and into her eyes, blurring her vision. Below the voices of the two men tending to Wren, a shrill hum rang in her ears as she fought to keep her knees from buckling. Concerned neighbors were milling about just outside the apartment door. She wanted to chase them off, scream at them to go away and mind their own business.

"Um, no, I can look around and see what I can find." Her voice sounded unfamiliar in her head; vacant and distant, but shockingly coherent.

She didn't have to look long. On the bathroom counter, in reach of little Iva, she found two prescription bottles—Adderall and Xanax. Each bottle held only a few pills. Neither had a secured lid. Angry heat rose in Birdie at Wren's carelessness. She stifled her rage and took the bottles to the paramedic. He thanked her and quickly lifted the gurney over the threshold to the awaiting ambulance. She jumped when the siren belted out its cry, shut the door, and returned to the bedroom to check on the kids. As the ambulance drove away with a groggy, but responsive Wren, anger prompted Birdie to call her parents. Roy and Lula would rush to Wren's side. She couldn't shield them from this episode. As for herself, she had no interest in checking on her younger sister. She packed bags for the kids and cleaned up Marlow. The infant barely stirred, content with a full belly and a dry diaper. As she secured Iva in her car seat, she asked her young niece in her most cheery voice, "How about we pick up a Happy Meal on the way to my house?"

The child said nothing in response; she simply nodded her head. Birdie saw tears building in the young girl's eyes.

"Mommy is going to be fine, sweetie," Birdie said, lovingly running her hands along Iva's matted braid and then wiping a single tear as it slid slowly down the girl's face.

In a small voice, Iva repeated, "Mommy's missing her show."

This would be the last time Iva responded to her mother's mayhem flatly. The child was in shock. As Birdie sat in the drive-thru and drove home, the resentment festered inside of her. How dare her sister put the children through something so traumatic?

What was to be a weekend stay continued for several weeks as Wren sought to shake her dependency on the two prescriptions that had allowed her to function. Jacob was busy shoring up the final details of his international trip to begin his new stint in Holland. The timing of it all was abysmal.

———

Wren exited rehab as if she'd been handed a clean slate. Again her firm belief was that she'd been the one who suffered, never acknowledging the toll the ordeal had taken on her family. She didn't apologize, simply expecting that they all forgive and forget. Wren had turned over another new leaf; therefore, she should be exalted for her efforts, and everyone in her orbit should move on.

"Give them some space, Birdie," Lula admonished as she poured two glasses of iced tea from a pitcher and carried them to the kitchen table where she sat and patted the seat next to her, urging Birdie to join her.

Lula continued, "It's so good to have her out of that place, but the work isn't over. We need to be there for your sister. I'll get you a schedule of the meetings. They even have a program for young children so Iva can be included; little Marlow is too young still. She can't recover from this without our support."

Birdie had heard all of this before. They would be expected to drop everything and attend meetings and therapy sessions to help Wren work through her issues.

"I'm not wasting another minute on Wren's recovery, Mom," Birdie said angrily, turning away from the scene that played out in the next room. She joined her mother at the kitchen table.

In the living room, Iva bombarded Wren with stories about what she had missed while she did another rehab stint. Iva chattered eagerly but made no mention of the sleepless nights, the tears, the tantrums that overwhelmed her and her baby brother. Neither her parents nor her sister acknowledged the fear and sadness the children struggled with while Birdie did her best to distract and reassure them that all would be fine.

"Now, Birdie, you know how important family involvement is to an addict's recovery. The doctors said—"

Birdie couldn't stand to hear it all again and cut her mother off.

"Really, Mom? We're important to her recovery? If that were true, we wouldn't be in this position right now, because we have done *everything* to support her how many times before this?" Birdie sat rigidly, red-faced, her elbows pressed hard into the table, her hands rubbing her forehead fiercely. "Maybe it's time to try another approach. Let's let Wren deal with it herself. Maybe then she will actually make a change!"

"Keep your voice down, Birdie," Lula said, peering over her daughter's shoulder, hoping Iva was too preoccupied to hear Birdie's angry voice.

"Why, Mom? So we don't upset fragile, little Wren? She doesn't seem too put out by any of this. Did she thank you for your help while she was gone? Did she offer up her concern or seem the slightest bit distressed that her children cried themselves to sleep every night? Does she care that she could have *died* and left them alone in that horrible apartment with her decaying body?

Does anyone get any of this?" Birdie ended her tirade with a frustrated groan, dropping her head to the table.

"Now, honey, I know you're upset, and I know this has been hard on all of us, but she's your sister—"

"I'm done, Mom. I suggest you avoid dragging those children to those godforsaken meetings! That is the last place they need to be. In fact, it'd be better for them to just stay on at my place. I'm sure Wren needs some time to adjust to the real world."

"Now you're just being ridiculous," Lula said. "They've missed out on enough time with their mother already. Things will be fine. Your father and I cleared out that apartment. She and the kids are going to be staying here with us for a while, until she can get back on her feet."

Birdie handed the children back over to their mother. Her only comfort in the act was knowing that the children would be afforded some measure of security under the watchful eyes of Roy and Lula.

Birdie returned to an empty home where the earthy outdoor scent of Iva, and the fresh baby powder aroma of Marlow, lingered in the air. Jacob's musk still rose from the pillow when she climbed into the bed they once shared.

Some nights she fought back tears while speaking to Jacob on the phone as she wallowed in her gloom. Some nights she didn't even answer his calls, unsure that she could hide her despondency as Jacob excitedly reported on how his day went, the breakthroughs he had with his students and his general giddiness with experiencing life in a foreign country. The calls came less and less often as he embraced his life overseas. His inquiries about when she would join him lost their ardor and eventually ceased. Birdie was always waiting for the other shoe to drop and knew she needed to be at home, near the children, when it did.

———

What started as a general conversation, a simple push for Wren to move forward, would prove consequential for the Clarksons.

"Euphemia, from my book club, mentioned that they need a receptionist at Parson Chiropractic. Euphemia is the office manager," Lula told Wren one day. She had waited a few weeks after Wren's discharge to bring up finding a job. "She said she has an interview spot open tomorrow at two o'clock."

"Well, that might just work. Maybe I can hook myself a doctor," Wren flippantly replied.

"Wear something appropriate and don't make me look bad, please Wren," Lula implored.

Wren was hired, thanks to Lula having a foot in the door, and a calm fell upon the Clarksons' world. They each held their breath, wondering how long it would last. But a little over a year before the snowstorm of 2011, Wren seemed to have made great strides. Her work at the chiropractor's office inspired her to take courses to become a massage therapist.

"I think she finally may be ready to settle down and do right," Lula told Birdie one day on the phone. "Your father and I are going to let them stay on here at the house a bit longer. Maybe she could save up enough to buy a small house for the kids. I don't want to see them back in one of those seedy apartments."

Birdie was more doubtful than her parents that a new job and housing arrangements would prove to be the things that settled Wren. She could still see the smoldering undercurrent in Wren's eyes, could sense the disquiet stirring in her younger sister's heart.

Chapter Six

2010 - WREN

He loved her; she knew he must. Why would he have let her in on his scheme to pilfer money from the clinic? To trust someone with that knowledge, it had to be love. Of course, he had told her he wasn't ready to leave his wife —his kids were too young. But Wren was confident it was only a matter of time.

She was ready to start a real life, leave behind her crazy days. She'd been sowing her oats far longer than most. A new life was long overdue. Time was etching itself on her once bright face, and weaving thinning silver strands into her hair. Victor Hall was her chance for that life. All she needed to do was follow his lead, play by his rules. He had a plan, and she was part of it.

It started as innocent flirtation. The kind of playful seduction that was a game for her.

"Wren, think you can help Euphemia out by taking the reins on those rejected claims? It might require some overtime, but she is struggling with the new software, and time's running out." He breezed into the clinic lobby, straightening his white lab coat. The intoxicating scent of his Herrera cologne filled the small space as he stood in front of her, leaning over the riser of the reception desk. He shot her a playful wink, and she noticed his gaze fell below her neckline.

"Certainly, Dr. Hall. Anything I can do to help," she replied, trying to maintain a professional pitch.

She must have failed, because she spotted Euphemia lean out around the corner where her desk sat. The aging woman was far out of her element, knew nothing about computers, and struggled with new coding regulations. However, she remained spry enough to sense the inappropriate undercurrent of the conversation taking place within her earshot. She peered over her thick glasses and clucked out a "Tsk!" before turning back to the mountain of paperwork threatening to take over her tidy desk.

That night was their first. Victor's wife was visiting her parents in Oklahoma City. But he didn't invite her to his home. It would be months before she saw where he lived. Their first tryst took place on a shaky exam table in the back storage room of the clinic. Wren never gave a thought to her children and their need for dinner and baths. Their grandparents could deal with those mundane tasks. As with all of Wren's moments, she was inside herself, absorbing the energy, relishing every sensation.

Wren and Dr. Hall became a thing—even if that

thing was only a passionate romp once a week at Parson Chiropractic and a rare nightcap at a dark bar. On Wednesday nights Victor's wife took his kids to church. There was never enough time in the day for the osteopath to grow his practice, or so he told his wife as he staved off invitations to join them for the midweek services. The Halls' church sat in plain view of the practice. Knowing her lover's wife sat in a pew directly across Duck Street gave Wren an even bigger thrill. The idea that Mrs. Hall could pop in on her way home and catch the two tangled together added to the exhilaration.

One night, as Wren eyed herself in the mirror, straightening her blouse and smoothing her hair, he made a proposal.

"I was wondering if you can keep a secret?"

She had to laugh. "Well, I've been keeping us a secret for a few months now."

"This is an even bigger secret," he whispered in her ear as he slid up behind her, wrapping his hands around her waist.

She looked at his reflection in the mirror. He was holding a wad of cash. His devastating smile seemed darker, almost menacing.

"What's that you got there, Dr. Hall?" she said teasingly, as she turned toward him and ran her fingers over the money.

"A ticket out of here," he replied, lifting her up onto the sink, money still in hand. Nuzzling his mouth into her neck, then to her ear, he whispered, "I'll never get my own practice with what Parson pays me, so I came up with a plan to compensate myself for what I'm worth. I won't be stuck as second fiddle for long."

His words sent shivers through her body.

Wren never gave a second thought to becoming an embezzler. She viewed herself as a co-conspirator.

———

To Victor, she was little more than a pawn—the perfect patsy. As he skimmed increasing sums off the coffers of the booming practice, Wren was drawn further into his ruse. She seemed oblivious to the peril she put herself in. Victor wasn't fully aware of Wren's lust for danger. He was impressed with some of her ideas and used her eagerness and finesse to his advantage, allowing him to amass more ill-gotten gains. He was smart enough to keep the money out of the banks and believed strongly that she would not betray him. She held all the evidence. If anyone noticed the money was missing, he could keep his hands clean, and he had no doubts about who would win in a he-said, she-said case.

"I keep it in my old suitcase, on my closet shelf. No one would think to look there. But if we keep this up, I'm gonna need a bigger suitcase," she told him one Wednesday night. They sat next to each other at the conference room table, too busy covering their tracks, discussing their next steps, to even bother getting undressed. She stroked his hand teasingly with her fingernails. His mind was so set on the need to cover his tracks that he barely registered the tingling chill her long, red nails left as they trailed across his skin.

"We won't need a bigger suitcase any time soon," he replied.

Victor's paranoia increased as quickly as the funds did. He had become fearful that Euphemia might be sniffing around, questioning the balance sheets. He loosened his tie and laid out phase two of his plan to Wren.

"It's time for us to sever our ties," he started.

Her hand froze on his, and a suspicious veil slipped over her gaze.

"Just to the outside world. It's only temporary."

Instantly, she withdrew her hand, and he saw the flicker of doubt and mistrust in her eyes. He changed course in hopes of keeping her on track.

"We both need to lie low. Just long enough for the battle-ax to move on to other pressing matters."

This seemed to mollify her briefly, until he said, "It'd be best if you could get yourself fired. It will look too suspicious if you quit."

Twenty-five thousand plus dollars missing could be explained away, especially if the promiscuous admin were to make a quick exit. He teetered on a thin wire, needing to keep her close enough to control the strings, but distancing himself so as not to become too entangled. He was keenly aware that one slip in timing or a misread cue could cause the whole scheme to unravel, leaving him vulnerable.

"Fired?" she said, pushing back from the table and shaking her head. "No, I can't get fired. My mom would disown me and I'm so close to getting my massage license."

He knew this was a lie. Her instructor was a patient of his who, during a manipulation months ago, had let it slip that Wren was less than a stellar student, who rarely attended class and had zero hours of hands-on practice under her belt.

"Euphemia is asking questions, talking about hiring an auditor. We need to let things blow over. Remember, it won't be long. The spinster has to be retiring someday soon," he said coolly, interjecting his own untruths.

————

While Wren wasn't happy about the turn of events, she was a master at getting herself fired. She felt a tinge of guilt lying to him about her failed efforts in massage school, but she had no concerns about her parent's expectations. They were used to her lousy career choices, and her courses had fallen by the wayside. She was too distracted by new love and the growing pile of cash in her closet. The way she saw it, she wouldn't need to be a masseuse once she became the next Mrs. Hall. Euphemia Jones had been looking for an excuse to can her since Dr. Parson hired her. The older woman made it clear she still believed a good work ethic and polite manners could bring new patients to the practice. She had never hidden her disdain about Dr. Parson stooping so low as to use a short skirt and low-cut top to lure in patrons and keep them coming back for more manipulations, both of ego and of spine.

Wren knew Euphemia's relationship with her mother was the only reason the spinster didn't raise a stink about Dr. Parson's choice. There was no doubt Euphemia regretted that decision every minute of the day. She never missed the opportunity to remind Wren how one should never mix business and friendship.

Wren took an odd, perverse thrill in getting under the woman's skin as she went about botching the calendar, jumbling appointments, and not delivering messages. It only took a week before these ploys became too much for her senior to tolerate. She wished she could have been a fly on the wall during the conversation Euphemia had with Dr. Parson. It was another game for Wren, barely a challenge.

"I'm sorry, Euphemia. Please give me another chance. I've been so preoccupied with my kids, and I think my dad may be taking ill—" Wren played the part impeccably and impressed herself with the falsehood regarding her father. Tears sprang forth effortlessly as Euphemia handed Wren her last paycheck and a small box to pack her belongings.

"Well, I am truly sorry to hear about Roy. Your parents are good people. But your oversights are affecting the patients. We can't afford to tarnish the Parson name with such carelessness," Euphemia replied sternly. "If you'll notice, Dr. Parson was very generous with your final check. Against my urging, he insisted I add a nice severance cushion that should tide you over for a bit."

Wren went about packing her things, snatching a tissue from the box on the desk as she did, dabbing her eyes and wiping her nose. She put on a good show.

"Do you think I could tell the doctors goodbye?" Wren asked when the last of her items were tucked into the box.

"I don't think that would be prudent. They are busy men and patients are waiting," Euphemia replied with finality.

Her tears stopped the instant the door swung closed behind her, leaving dried streams that cut through her makeup. She got in her car and the song "Bye Bye Bye" was playing on the radio. She giggled at the irony while she hummed along with the tune as she drove away from the clinic.

Her carefree mood faded as days passed without hearing from Victor. It wasn't long before she started placing calls to the clinic, disguising her voice or trying to reach him after hours, on Wednesday nights. She even dared to call his house several times, concealing her identity from his caller I.D. by dialing *67 before his phone number; then holding her breath for a few seconds when Mrs. Hall answered, always hanging up without saying a word.

Wren's desperation mounted as her partner in crime effortlessly avoided her.

Chapter Seven

Around the time that Wren was working on getting herself fired, Birdie found herself picking up the slack again. Wren was too preoccupied with something in her day-to-day to dedicate much time to her own children. Birdie often took Iva and Marlow on the weekends, giving her parents a much-needed break from tending to the energetic twosome.

"Your sister is so busy with her classes. She's hardly ever here," Lula told Birdie.

"Glad to see her finally applying herself, you know?" Roy chimed in as he handed her the kids' overnight bags.

Birdie smiled and nodded, never believing that Wren's absence was due to something so virtuous. She kept her doubts to herself because she didn't have the heart to squelch their hopes.

Most single, professional women might spend their

free time socializing, looking for love, just about anything, really, besides fawning over two children who weren't theirs. But Birdie relished her time with Iva and Marlow. Their weekends together were more for her than they ever were for Lula and Roy.

Still, Lula fussed and concerned herself with Birdie's after-hours choices.

"You should join my book club, Birdie," Lula pressed. "Well, you should really join a singles club or try online dating, but at least the book club would get you out of your house. Maybe one of the book club ladies has a nice nephew, or an acquaintance they could introduce you to."

Birdie knew arguing with her mother would get her nowhere, and secretly she did admit to herself that was she dangerously close to becoming a friendless bore. But at the first book club meeting she attended, her notion that her sister wasn't on the path of the straight and narrow was unexpectedly supported.

The weekly get-together was more of a competition of who had the juiciest gossip than a true forum to discuss the literary selection. Birdie sat quietly in Euphemia's fussy sitting room as the group of women tried to outdo each other, seeing who had the most scandalous dirt to dish. Her ears perked up when Euphemia started talking about the young chiropractor at her clinic and her suspicions that he was a serial cheater. Euphemia didn't offer much evidence to support her claim, but

Birdie was aware that the woman felt quite confident in her assessment of the man.

As the group continued to chatter about who was getting divorced, children who had dropped out of college, house foreclosures, and the ills of small-town life, Birdie went to the kitchen to top off her cup of decaf. As she turned away from the coffee pot, she found herself face-to-face with the stern Euphemia; the woman stood so close, Birdie almost spilled coffee on the older woman's poly-blend blazer.

"Oh, sorry, you startled me. Just getting more coffee," Birdie stammered.

"I didn't want to say anything in front of your mother, dear," Euphemia said in a hushed voice. She glanced from side to side, making sure the two were alone, and her eyes narrowed to slits. "I do believe your sister is Dr. Hall's latest extramarital conquest."

Birdie stood dumbfounded as Euphemia skirted around her and added a lady finger to her saucer before topping her cup off as well.

"She is sure to bring shame to our prestigious prac-tice. How I wish she had never been hired," Euphemia said, speaking out of the side of her mouth; brushing past Birdie and returning to the group scuttlebutt taking place in the formal living room.

Birdie was flustered by the news. She didn't doubt that Wren could likely be engaged in a furtive affair with the chiropractor, but she was unsure of Euphemia's motive in divulging the information. She tried to push her concerns out of her mind and join the group, which had now begun discussing the novel, but she couldn't concentrate on the conversation. A sense of foreboding flooded her mind.

———

It didn't take long for Euphemia's claim and Birdie's concern to prove valid. A few nights after the book club meeting, Birdie forced herself to accept an invitation to join her colleagues for a drink after work. The group had just settled in at a high-top table and placed their orders when Birdie spotted her sister. Wren sat in a dark, corner booth with a man, pressed closely against him and twirling a lock of his hair around her manicured finger. The fool still had his wedding ring on but made every attempt to keep his back to the early Friday night crowd. Birdie knew her sister didn't notice her staring over her glass of Chardonnay. Unable to focus on her colleagues' banter, she was fixated on the oblivious couple. Her thoughts were consumed with worry about this illicit rela-tionship, and she dreaded what it could mean to the status quo the family was enjoying. It wasn't until Wren and her date got up to leave that Birdie recognized the man as the new chiropractor from the clinic where Wren worked. She'd seen his image on billboards around town. Birdie's cheeks flushed with anger that Wren would compromise their mother's efforts and friendship by getting entangled with a married man, a coworker no less. She excused herself to splash cold water on her face in the lady's room.

———

Birdie did her best to console her mother as she lamented about Wren losing yet another job; this one especially since she had put her friendship on the line for it. With great doubt, she told her mom that Euphemia wouldn't hold it against her and scoffed at Lula's fears that she would be booted from the book club. Birdie dropped the words, "I told you so," from her conversations with her parents some time ago, although it had been difficult; and seeing her mother so troubled compelled her to bite her tongue again ... hard.

The following week, Birdie was happy to see that Euphemia greeted Lula with all the warmth the woman could ever muster. As the book club ladies were getting comfortable and withdrawing the week's book out of their tote bags, the chatter had already begun.

"Well, none of them wanted to take care of his old dog when he went into rehab after his stroke. That dog was all poor Wilson had since his wife passed. His sister took the old mutt to the pound and told her brother that the dog had died!"

Tsks and clucks spread through the small group, who sat on the edge of their plastic-covered seats.

"That's simply monstrous," replied Roselyn Grant, as she reached for a lemon bar.

"That poor dog," muttered Betsy Landers, shaking her head.

"Poor man," cried Rosa Suarez. "Who could do such a thing to family?"

No one had time to reply to the question. The group's hostess, Euphemia, straightened her spine, cleared her throat, and said, "I believe someone has embezzled money from the clinic."

A gasping hush resonated through the room. Just like that, the gossipy group forgot all about the heartless Brenna Shull and her ailing brother's dog. This was by far the richest tidbit ever disclosed at the book club. The women placed their books in their laps and leaned forward, eager to learn more.

Birdie had been ignoring the chatter by fiddling with her new phone. Her attention was captured immediately by the change of subject. As Euphemia spilled the details of the misfortune that had fallen upon the Parson Clinic, her eyes never looked away from Birdie.

Birdie shifted in her seat and plucked a piece of lint off her skirt as the heat of Euphemia's glare made her cheeks flush. She pulled three tissues from the box on the side table next to her. She dabbed her forehead and cheeks, blotting away tiny beads of sweat. Lula sat next to her daughter, enthralled by the telling and oblivious to the insinuation Euphemia was making. Lula leaned into Birdie and whispered, "Guess it's a good thing your sister isn't working there any longer."

What brought Lula relief provoked fear and distress

that Birdie felt in her gut. For the remainder of the evening, Birdie wasn't aware of the conversations that spun around her; it was all white noise. She was inside her own head, piecing together pieces of the puzzle and fretting about what it all meant. This could be Wren's most consequential catastrophe yet.

Chapter Eight

For over three weeks Victor did not take Wren's calls, but she kept trying. One evening, with trembling hands and tears in her eyes, she dialed his phone and waited for it to go to voicemail. She never left a message but would listen to his voice, hanging up before he finished his sign-off. Only this time, he picked up. For a second she didn't believe he'd actually answered. She brushed the tears from her face, took a deep breath, and said, "Victor?"

"Listen, you need to stop calling me," he said in a harsh whisper. "I told you I would be in touch when the time was right. You are going to ruin everything if you can't keep it together a while longer. My wife is getting suspicious about all the hang-up calls. Get a grip!"

"I know. I just miss you and..." She was sobbing again. She hated being so pathetic. But hearing his voice awakened her senses. She saw her world growing gray in his absence but connecting with him again brought color back in a way that shocked her.

In the background she could hear a woman's voice and the laughter of children. She closed her eyes and imagined herself in that world. The mirage faded quickly.

"It's nothing, hon. One of those annoying robocalls."

He ended the call without a goodbye. The silence shrouded her in betrayal and abject loneliness. Never had she felt so hopeless and rejected.

She threw her phone onto the bed and collapsed to her knees. No sound escaped her lips as her face turned red, flush with overwhelming emotions that left her feeling spent and desperate. She fell into a troubled sleep there on the floor of her childhood bedroom. When she woke, her hair stuck to her face in sweaty tendrils, trapped in the lines left by her dried tears; and her shoulder ached from lying on the wood floor. Sleep did not quiet her discontent; and as she got to her feet, a plan rose and took shape in her mind. She knew what she could do to quell the overwhelming fear of being alone, of losing again.

She went to her closet and grabbed the suitcase off the shelf. Unable to fully acknowledge the emerging plan, she slid on her shoes and slung her purse over her shoulder. If she allowed herself to think, courage would be lost. Lightning flashed in the windows outside her bedroom and booming thunder shook the house. She paid no mind to the mounting storm outside as she descended the attic stairs and placed the suitcase in the hallway outside the room where her children slept. It was late. The house was dark and quiet. She tip-toed to Iva's bed first and roused the young girl from her sleep.

"Come with Mommy," Wren whispered, taking Iva's hand.

Iva didn't question her mother's request. Her bare feet slapped on the wooden floors, as she rubbed her eyes and followed Wren blindly to Marlow's bed. Wren scooped up the sleeping child and shushed him as he stirred.

She led Iva down the stairs while she struggled with the suitcase and sleeping child in her arms. They stopped briefly in the laundry room. Wren put the suitcase down and opened the refrigerator door. She spotted the box of wine on the bottom shelf and handed it to Iva.

"Carry this for Mommy, sweetie," she whispered.

Iva did as she was told.

"Open the door too, baby," Wren whispered to her daughter.

"Where are we going, Mommy? I don't have my shoes. It's raining,"

"Just going for a ride; you won't need your shoes. Now go on, hurry up. Get the door for me. Your brother weighs a ton."

Wren's red Hyundai was parked in the garage. Her ever-chivalrous father had given up his spot when she moved in with the children. She groped blindly until her hand found the button on the wall. She didn't bother buckling Marlow into his car seat and told Iva to get in the front while she placed the suitcase in the trunk. The young girl couldn't hide the surprise on her face as she dutifully did what her mother told her to do.

Wren saw her daughter struggling with the buckle in the front seat and realized why her child seemed so apprehensive.

"See, you're a big girl now. So big, you get to sit in the front seat with me."

"You forgot to buckle Marlow in, Mommy," Iva said quietly, fighting tears.

"Why are you crying?" Wren questioned the girl, unable to hide her mounting frustration. "I thought you'd like sitting up here with me."

"But Aunt Birdie says little kids belong in the backseat." The child was worked up now; gasping sobs broke her speech.

"Oh, yeah, right," a distracted Wren replied. "It's okay, we aren't going far."

"I'll sit in the back with Marlow," the child said as she climbed over the center console. She quickly buckled her brother's car seat as best she could; then settled into her space and secured her belt as well.

"Suit yourself," Wren hissed as she put the car in gear.

"You need to buckle too, Mommy."

"Yep, right again, Iva," Wren snapped, reaching for her belt and buckling it as she reversed the car out of the garage.

It had been an unseasonably warm start to winter. A light rain was falling. In the distance the clouds lit up with erratic flashes of lightning.

She knew where Victor lived—had driven past his home on numerous occasions just to be closer to him, perhaps glimpse him through a window. She drove straight to his house and boldly parked at the end of his driveway. Iva and Marlow had fallen asleep during the short ride.

Wren found a Mexico Joe's cup in her cup holder. It was halfway full of flat soda. She rolled the window down, dumped the cup's remains onto her lover's manicured lawn, and filled the tumbler with wine; then washed down a Xanax with the bitter drink. She wasn't sure how long she sat and stared at the house—walking its halls in her mind, imagining herself being the woman who resided there with Victor, sleeping beside him in the bed. She deserved it more than his wife did. She'd sacrificed so much to protect the man, to lay the foundation of their life together. Now, it was all slipping away from her. The plan solidified, and she decided to carry out the act that would deny Victor of his ill-gotten gains and his chance at a life with her. The time had come to erase all her pain and absolve her children of the shame and uncertainty they would be subjected to if she left them behind.

Knowing she would need a bit more liquid courage to go through with it, she quickly downed another cup of the wine. The tires of her tiny car spun on the wet street as she pulled away from the home, the life that might have been.

She drove aimlessly through the quiet streets of downtown Stillwater, barely acknowledging to herself that she did have a final destination. Once she found herself traveling south on I-177, she floored it, pushing the small car to a speed she didn't know it was capable of. It wasn't long before she spotted what she was looking for … a lone eighteen-wheeler lumbering its way toward the college town. As the truck ambled closer, she turned off the windshield wipers to blur her vision in hopes of obscuring the last terrifying sight she would see. When the truck grew nearer, she jerked the steering wheel to the left and closed her eyes. Iva's screams competed with the air horn of the truck as the driver braked hard.

Behind the wheel of his rig, the driver struggled to keep the truck on the road, silently praying that the tread of his wheels stayed connected to the wet blacktop. The car came out of nowhere. It was small and traveling fast. It stood no chance against his enormous truck that was weighed down with bricks. Just as he was certain he was about to unwillingly kill someone, the tiny car veered off the road, landing in the culvert on the opposite side of the highway. He gave an angry blast of his horn, and mumbled to himself, "Crazy, drunk college kids," as he continued on. He wasn't going to stop for the vehicle that almost changed his life in unfathomable ways. He drove on, counting his blessings while cursing the unknown driver.

The car came to a jolting stop in the ditch. Wren still grasped the steering wheel, breathing so heavily she couldn't calm her children. She didn't know how long it took for her breath to grow steady and her heart rate to slow. Her pulse pounded in her ears, making her oblivious to her children's cries. She was angry with herself for chickening out.

"Mommy, he's bleeding!"

Iva's screams finally drowned out the pulsing ring inside her head. The child was crying hysterically.

Marlow had slipped down in the car seat, which hadn't been tightened enough by Iva's small hands. His little neck took the brunt of the force and the nylon belt dug deeply into his skin. The young boy's cries were silent. Shock, pain, and terror stole his breath, choking out his ability to make noise.

"It's okay, Marlow. Let me see where you're bleeding from." She frantically pushed her son's long hair back, searching for the source of the stream of blood. She desperately hoped the damage was minimal and was relieved to see that the wound wasn't as bad as she feared; more of a burn inflicted by the coarse material.

Iva continued to wail.

"Iva, he's fine. It isn't bad. Are you hurt somewhere?"

The sobbing child shook her head.

"Hold this napkin to your brother's neck then, so I can get us out of here."

She turned the key, and the car made a grinding noise, telling her it was still running. She put the car in reverse. The tires spun helplessly in the thick red mud as she tried to back out of the ditch. She kept trying but realized she was only making matters worse. It would be impossible to keep this failed fool's errand a secret. She found her purse on the front floorboard and dug through it until her hand landed on her phone.

"Daddy, I need help. I've been in a little accident with the kids."

———

Birdie rose from the table where she sat drinking coffee with her mother. "She did what?"

"Now, don't make a mountain out of a molehill, Bird."

Lula's hands shook as she placed the mug on the table. Her face was drawn; dark shadows lay heavy under her puffy eyes. Birdie could see that despite her mother's attempts to make light of the situation, she was frazzled, frightened even, by the event. Exasperation kept Birdie from offering a comforting hug to her mother,

"Mom, how is driving in the middle of the night, intoxicated, with your children anything but a mountain?"

"Marlow will be fine. It's a rug burn from the car seat strap."

"She could have killed them!"

"Oh, stop being so dramatic," Lula urged her daughter.

Birdie paced around the kitchen. "Did she explain to you *why* she decided to chug some wine, pop a pill or two, and take her kids on a blitzed-out joyride at three o'clock in the morning, in the rain no less?"

"She said she needed to clear her head."

"Clear her head? Since when has she had anything even close to a 'clear head?' And it seems she could 'clear her head' better without waking two young children to join her on her 'head clearing' mission!"

"Birdie, stop. She is their mother. She has the right to take them anywhere she wants." Lula's tone was harsh, admonishing. Her voice was shaky.

The sun broke through the morning clouds; a beam of light shone from the window and fell across Lula's face as a tear slipped down her cheek. Birdie sensed that her mother's anger was more towards her than Wren. This awareness deepened the divide, making her believe she was the foe, that the issue lay with her. She wished she could walk away and end the maddening conversation right then, but she pushed on.

"You're joking, right? I can't believe you are defending her! She is a danger to those kids, and this isn't the first time she's put their lives at risk! What does Dad say about Wren's latest debacle?"

"Well, he wasn't pleased, but——"

"Let me guess…" Birdie put her hand on the table and leaned in close to her mother's face. "He paid to have her car towed. That'll teach her!"

"No, he was able to pull her car out with his truck." Lula's gaze did not meet Birdie's intense stare.

"Of course!" Birdie said, turning away from the table and resuming her frenzied pacing. "Wren stirs up an insane amount of chaos but gets herself out of it scot-free! Why would I expect anything different?" She threw her hands up, ignoring the coffee that spilled down her arm.

"Her car did suffer some damage. Your father told Wren he wouldn't pay for the repairs."

"Oh, well, then. Poor Wren!" Birdie took her mother's coffee cup and went to the pot, topping off both cups before returning to her seat at the kitchen table. She took a deep breath, willing her pulse to slow; welcoming the brief silence as she tried to regain her composure, more for her mother's sake than her own.

"Where is everyone?" She asked, forcing herself to keep her voice calm. "Have you checked Marlow's neck? Does he need to see a doctor?"

"He's fine, Birdie. No doctor needed. Just some Neosporin and a bandage. He and Wren are asleep. Your dad took Iva to school. She didn't want to miss her class winter party."

"Well, hopefully she can stay awake since her mother kept her out all night."

Wren entered the kitchen, still in a bathrobe, her hair disheveled. She grabbed a large coffee mug from the cabinet and went directly to the coffee pot. "Good morning to you, dear sister. If you came to save the day again, you're late. All is well."

"It's already afternoon and if I could save those kids from you, believe me, I would." Birdie's heart rate hadn't begun to return to normal before her sister's comments sent it skyrocketing again.

"Do you need help getting down from your high horse?" Wren said snidely, as she shuffled to the kitchen table, taking a seat across from Birdie. She pulled her phone out of the robe pocket and began swiping through her notifications.

"You don't deserve those kids! And worse yet, they don't deserve a mess like you! How dare you, Wren? They could have died. Do you get that? Do you understand what could have happened?" Birdie slammed both hands on the table and kept them there to stop them from trembling as she pressed closer to her sister. "If you wanted to end your own pathetic life, so be it! But Iva and Marlow? I don't understand—" Now her whole body trembled with rage and couldn't find the words to continue.

"Birdie!" Lula warned.

Wren looked up from her phone, locking eyes with Birdie in a heartless, cold stare. Her voice was stony and smooth.

"I took them with me because I'll never let you have them. You'll never be their mother. You'll never be anyone's mother."

"Wren!" Lula whispered, the shock and anguish drawn on her face.

Her sister's callousness left Birdie seething. She tossed her coffee into the kitchen sink and rinsed her cup. Then she grabbed her purse and keys and left the house without another word, letting the slamming door speak for her.

On her drive to campus, thoughts of Wren's carelessness and the implications for Iva and Marlow consumed her. Something needed to be done to help her niece and nephew before their mother could wreak more havoc on their young lives. Of course, she knew it was pointless to think that way. She was helpless to stop the tears of frustration and anger. When she pulled into a parking spot, she checked her face in the mirror and saw a blotchy reddened mess punctuated with running mascara. She felt exhausted and looked worse, so she decided to forgo office hours and drove home, where she spent the rest of the day watching holiday movies on television while wrapping Christmas gifts. The cheery activities did nothing to lift her spirits. When she crawled into bed that night, feeling beyond spent, she believed she would sleep well. Instead, she lay awake, tossing and turning, stressing over her plight—about all she had sacrificed in the interest of Iva and Marlow, and about being tortured by her sister's inability to see how fortunate she was.

Chapter Nine

2011

After two weeks of hearing nothing from Wren, the Clarkson family grew to believe the flighty woman wouldn't be returning anytime soon. Birdie struggled to comfort and reassure the children that all was well. Iva was mournful in the wake of her mother's exit. The young girl cried herself to sleep almost every night, constantly questioning where her mother had gone, unable to understand why she had left. Marlow lashed out at anything in his path and was sent home early from preschool more days than not. The school's director was sympathetic to the situation, but Birdie feared it wouldn't be long before he was told to leave for good. He never asked about his mother's whereabouts.

Concern and anger got the best of Lula, and she convinced Roy to hire a private investigator. They never did report their daughter missing to authorities. She had obviously left of her own accord, having taken her suitcase and personal items with her. Her voicemail box filled up quickly after the discovery that she was gone. It only rang for a few hours after the sun came up that day; after that, it went straight to a message saying the mailbox was full.

The investigator, Liam Klarus, asked Roy and Lula to obtain their daughter's phone records; Wren had been on their wireless plan since first getting a mobile phone. The phone records provided scant clues as to Wren's mysterious departure.

All three Clarksons gathered at the dining room table two months after Wren left, eagerly awaiting information from Mr. Klarus. Birdie sat quietly eyeballing the man, unable to determine his age and wondering where her parents had found the P.I. He looked exactly as she would expect an investigator to look, aside from his attire; a bit haggard, his eyes shone with a wisdom that made her feel like he could see into her very soul. Deep lines on his tanned face gave him the appearance of a man who spent many hours in a car, chain-smoking and drinking from a large thermos of black coffee. Instead of the tweed pants and a button-down she believed he should be wearing, Mr. Klarus wore crisply ironed Wranglers and a western shirt complete with mother-of-pearl snaps.

"Well, folks, your daughter received a text message the night she left," the man told them.

He pushed a piece of paper across the table; the text

was highlighted in blue. Roy was first to pick up the only piece of evidence Mr. Klarus seemed to have. He read the message out loud to the group, "It's time. Meet me at thirty-second and Range at midnight. Bring the money." His tone rose with each word, making the statement sound like a question. He passed it to Lula who read the message to herself before sliding it across the table to Birdie. When Birdie finished reading it, she looked to the detective and asked, "Okay, so who sent the text? It stands to reason that she would be with this person."

"None of that makes sense. Wren didn't have any money," Roy said quietly.

"I can't speak to her finances, sir. You'd need a court order for that," the detective replied. "And, yes, I agree, ma'am. The message strongly implies that she left with the sender. The problem is whoever sent that text used a burner phone."

"What's a burner phone?" asked Lula, taking the piece of paper from her daughter and rereading the message.

"It's an untraceable phone. There's not enough information available for me to find out who sent the text. People buy the phones off the streets sometimes. For obvious reasons, they are often used by folks up to no good."

"So, what does that mean? We are nowhere closer to any answers," Roy said. His shaky voice betrayed his anger and frustration.

"I'm afraid I've hit a dead end. If you wanted to file a missing person report with the police, they may be able to compel more details. But I gotta tell you, a missing forty-something, who left obvious signs that she's gone by choice, isn't going to be high on the list of priorities for law enforcement."

"Thank you for your help, Mr. Klarus. We can settle up in my den," Roy said, rising and directing the man across the home's entry hall.

Lula and Birdie sat at the table in silence. Tears pooled in Lula's eyes, threatening to spill down her face.

"I don't understand. What money? I mean, she said she got a severance from the clinic. She did buy some pricey Christmas gifts for the kids, but I just thought she used that money. That maybe she was trying to make amends for the night she…"

Lula trailed off. Birdie knew her mother couldn't bring herself to speak of the night Wren almost got her children and herself killed. Her mother collected herself and surprised Birdie with her next question.

"You don't think…?"

"No, Mom. Wren's too full of herself to end her life. What she did that night was just another one of her attention-getting schemes. She'll be back. She always comes back," Birdie said, doubting that she sounded convincing.

"She's never been gone this long, Bird. And when she does leave, she usually gets in touch, checks on the kids, something."

"You and I both know there is no rhyme or reason to anything Wren does. She's always been tight-lipped, deceptive even. She could have run off with anyone. You're certain she didn't mention anyone she was seeing? Have you asked Iva or Marlow?"

"I don't want to upset those poor kids any further. I've hinted around; they're as oblivious as the rest of us. Iva says her mom lives in the forest now, which makes no sense. Maybe it's the only way her young mind can cope. I catch her standing at this window, staring out at the woods. Sometimes she even waves. Waves at nothing, Birdie. There is no one there." Lula's tone took on a pleading quality that only angered Birdie more.

"If it was a man and there was money involved, as this mystery text implies, he'll tire of her eventually, or she'll get bored with him, the money will run out, and she'll come back without a care in the world, probably sooner rather than later. Let's hope she hasn't finally sent her children over the deep end. If Iva has created an imaginary friend in the form of her missing mother, well, who knows … therapy, counseling."

Lula's attempts to stave off tears failed, and they slid down her face freely. Thinking of what this might mean to Iva and Marlow brought tears of anger to Birdie's eyes as well, and she wiped them away defiantly.

Birdie had yet to broach the subject of Wren's relationship with the married chiropractor. Her mother wasn't ready to accept that truth, so Birdie kept the information to herself. Obviously her mother's mind had not gone to the place her mind did. She couldn't help but think of Euphemia's claims of an embezzler at the clinic. Could that be the money the text message spoke of? Even if it were true, Roy and Lula would never accept the idea; and without proof of any of it, Birdie would only look spiteful and accusatory.

"I don't know, it feels different this time," Lula replied, staring out the window. "I hear movement up in the attic every night. When it wakes me, I think she must have come home, but when I go to her room, it's empty."

"Do you want me to take the kids to my place? They can stay there for a bit. I've lined up some showings with a realtor this weekend. Maybe if I took them house hunting, it'd get their minds off things."

Neither woman saw Iva. The young girl stood in the doorway of the dining room silently listening to the exchange but could not hold her tongue any longer.

"No, I want to stay here and wait for Mommy! She *does* live in the woods, I promise! She showed me!" the child exclaimed before turning and fleeing. Her footsteps echoed through the house as she ran up the stairs and slammed her bedroom door.

"We need to be careful what we say around them, Bird!" Lula admonished.

"Right, Mom, *we* need to be careful. Their own mother has never been careful with their feelings or even their very lives; but *we* need to be careful. We should just be up-front with them. I think they're old enough to understand what a colossal flake their mother is.

Tiptoeing around the subject and pretending everything is copacetic isn't going to fly much longer." Birdie was done with the niceties, done walking on eggshells. "I'd like to get a lawyer and start working toward permanent guardianship of the Iva and Marlow."

"Oh, Birdie, I think that's a bit premature. We don't know where she is or when she'll be back. We can't just cut her off without knowing what's going on."

"Okay, Mom, you keep your head in the sand. We'll leave those poor kids in limbo. Maybe your Detective Clouseau, or whatever his name is, will find some answers. Knowing Wren, she probably won the lottery and took off to some tropical island, so she didn't have to share it or take responsibility for her own life. Why should she? She knows we'll all be here to deal with the aftermath!"

Birdie delivered her outburst as she gathered her purse and jacket. Mr. Klarus and her dad were in the entryway. Roy was opening the front door for the investigator when Birdie pushed past them, heading to the roundabout where her car was parked.

"Have a good evening," she hissed as she crossed the threshold. When she reached her car, she looked back at the stunned men. "Dad, I wouldn't pour any more money into this useless venture. Wren doesn't care about us or her children. She's gone and she wanted to be gone. Let it go!"

She got in her car and sat for a few minutes before starting it. Her hands were shaking, and she didn't bother to wipe away the hot tears that streamed down her face. She pounded the steering wheel and let out a frustrated groan before struggling to get the key in the ignition. As she checked the mirror, she saw her sister sitting in the back seat. She was tending to the bundle she held, busying herself with the folds of the blanket.

"Go away! You wanted to leave, so leave," she shouted in the empty car. As she put the car in gear and hit the gas, she glanced over to see her dad looking apologetically at Mr. Klarus. Back in the mirror, she saw that her sister hadn't left. She was still there, her eyes gazing at the gray, winter landscape, her arms gently bobbing up and down, bouncing the bundle in her arms.

———

In the weeks and months following the private investigator's revelation, Roy Clarkson put countless miles on his old pickup truck traversing the dusty gravel roads that surrounded Camelot Crossing. He ended each rambling search at the desolate intersection believed to be the location his daughter was directed to in the cryptic text. He was never sure what it was he was looking for on the overgrown, forgotten paths, but whenever he spotted something that looked out of place, he'd hop out of his F-250 and grab his walking stick. As he poked through the weeds, he picked up more carelessly discarded fast food and convenience store litter and stumbled upon more roadkill that he ever thought possible, but never came upon anything that might reveal any hints of his daughter's whereabouts. His doggedness waned as Oklahoma's unpredictable spring gave way to its unforgiving summer. He abandoned his efforts, but never abandoned hope of Wren's eventual return.

Chapter Ten

IN BETWEEN

The next four years brought dramatic changes for the Clarksons. Birdie bought a three-bedroom house with a small home office a few miles from Camelot Crossing. Iva and Marlow moved in with her, and she became their guardian. Birdie continued to struggle with visions of Wren. So consumed by them at times, she considered seeking counseling in hopes of an explanation for her unsettling conjurings, but she never did. She couldn't shake the fear that doing so, confessing out loud to someone, might cause the mask to slip. If that happened, she could lose the kids; could even end up being a patient at one of the facilities Wren sought sanctuary in when life got hard. The idea of emulating her sister's behavior was unfathomable.

A new episode of *As the World Turns* greeted her each time she turned on a television. And while she realized the channel didn't exist in her cable lineup, she never explored an explanation. She felt relieved to realize she could simply change the channel to dismiss the program. The show aired endlessly on the nonexistent station, never breaking for commercials. The awareness that the phenomenon couldn't be a delusion of her own psyche perched itself just outside of her consciousness. There had to be a rational explanation, a rogue television wave or such.

One Saturday while she was under the weather, however, she sat in rapt attention to the program as it played out. Birdie was determined to interpret the parable. A new episode in the queue began rolling the second the closing credits faded to black on the previous one. None of them played out in sequential order. The changes in fashion and hairstyles were glaring, as were the characters who were killed off, and then resurrected through laughable ingenuity. She jotted down notes in an effort to make any correlations to Wren or the family's situation. But there was no solving the riddle; and after several hours of viewing, she nodded off in a cold medicine haze, only to awaken to yet another episode of the long-lost show and Iva standing over her.

"Why are you watching bee fights, Aunt Birdie?" the girl asked.

"What do you mean, bee fights?"

"The stuff on the television … it sounds like bees fighting, all buzzy, don't you think?"

"Oh, um sure, bee fights. The proper word is static. I don't know, maybe I rolled over on the clicker while I was napping," she replied, reaching for the remote to change the channel. Birdie didn't see visual static on the screen; she saw a black-and-white episode of a man and woman sharing knowing glances while tinny organ music expressed the tension of the scene and added to the cheesy melodrama that grated on Birdie's nerves.

Iva shrugged and walked back to her bedroom, leaving Birdie to doubt her long-held belief that the ready access to the soap opera was not a figment of her imagination. Wasting a day on the couch enthralled in a passé program brought her no closer to deciphering the message she believed was being sent to her. She vowed to give up on the futile effort.

She no longer bothered making her bed. Every evening when she arrived back home, the bed would be disheveled regardless of how she left it. It was easier to leave the bed a mess than believe that she was subconsciously sabotaging her own attempts of keeping a tidy room. Instead, she made the beds of Iva and Marlow each day to satisfy her neatnik compulsion. The children's beds always remained neatly fixed until they climbed into them each night.

She even resorted to keeping only the bare minimum pairs of shoes needed to get her through a season. It didn't have the effect she had hoped for. She still found shoes in her bedroom doorway at random times. But for some strange reason, she believed it lessened the frequency of the event. It gave her a sense of being in control, at least somewhat, of what she believed to be her fragile mental state. If the visions and inexplicable occurrences were indeed delusions of her stressed psyche or something much more aberrant, she knew that Wren was to blame. Somehow, even in her absence, her younger sister still held sway over her.

Birdie tried to find something to fill her life besides the kids and her job. But she dodged the occasional invitation from a male coworker to grab dinner or see a movie. Iva and Marlow weren't very accepting of men in Birdie's world. As the children grew older, they understood more and believed a man was to blame for their mother being gone. The children and their well-being were her top priority for the time being. It wouldn't be forever, she told herself. They would move on, move out, and have lives of their own. Maybe she could find companionship in her later years when she didn't have so much on her plate. Maybe she would never find someone worthy of filling Jacob's shoes.

She took over the book club when Euphemia stepped down after suffering a mild stroke. Though the original members came and went, most were still considerably older than her. They didn't try to set her up with bachelor family or friends, nor did they flood every conversation with talk of motherhood and marriage. They were all past that stuff, and that suited Birdie just fine. Birdie considered the group of elders to be her closest friends and confidants, yet she kept them all well beyond arm's length.

She volunteered as much as she could at Iva and

Marlow's primary school, Westwood Elementary, where conversations rarely strayed from parenting and marital woes. Marlow begged her to stop volunteering and not attend PTA meetings. Birdie knew that he was tired of explaining to people that his aunt, the woman who took care of him and shared his last name, was not his mother. Birdie didn't know how to help him, because he was unable to accept that his mother had abandoned him.

The rest of Birdie's time was devoted to her teaching and her parents. Roy's health was failing. By 2015, when Lula forced him to go to the doctor, the news was worse than any of them imagined. He had prostate cancer. The stubborn man had denied and ignored the symptoms so long that the cancer spread, first to his liver, then rapidly to his bones.

During the last summer of Roy Clarkson's life, his small family spent most of their time at the house in Camelot Crossing. Iva and Marlow worked on their tans poolside, while Birdie helped her mother care for Roy. The presence of death lurked just below the forced smiles and false hope. Birdie pushed family time—game night, movie night, puzzle night. Lula cooked all of Roy's favorite foods nightly, and always had a dessert to top it off—peach cobbler, lemon meringue pie, strawberry shortcake. All the efforts to squeeze in one more round of charades tired Roy more than he would let on; and most nights, his wife's amazing meals were left uneaten on his plate.

"I'm so grateful for all you and your mother are

doing to keep my spirits up," Roy said one night as Birdie helped him into bed.

"Nonsense, Dad—"

"No, now hear me out. I appreciate and love you all more than you could ever fathom." Roy struggled for breath, which worried Birdie, but she could tell he needed to get something off his chest.

"I feel like a selfish man, asking for anything more than what I've already been blessed with," he continued. "But I do wish I knew what happened to your sister. I hate the thought of leaving this world without knowing. Guess I've never been able to believe that she took off. Wondering why she left. Were we not good enough for her? Did we do something to push her away? It's never made any sense to me."

Birdie fluffed Roy's pillows, eased him back, and straightened his blankets, pulling them up to his shoulders. All the while, her mind searched for a way to respond. She was ashamed of the anger that stayed locked behind her clenched teeth. Still unsure of what words would spill out, she opened her mouth to speak but was relieved to see her father had nodded off. She bent down, kissed his forehead, and left the room, dimming the lights before closing the door.

Chapter Eleven

2015

Later that night, Birdie was startled awake by a familiar, but troubling sound. She sat up in bed and pushed the blankets off her legs, the sheets clinging to her skin thanks to the heavy humidity that threatened a drenching summer rain. A window air conditioner whirred loudly, and a ceiling fan spun furiously above her head. Neither was loud enough to block out the yowling that had awakened her as they struggled in tandem with the central air to cool the attic room on hot, sticky summer nights like tonight.

She sat motionless, her ears listening for the unusual sound that woke her. Just as she convinced herself that she was hearing things, a mournful mewl punctured the hum of the overworked cooling units. It was Cheshire. The cat refused to enter the attic room that still held all of Wren's belongings. She couldn't blame the cat. She, too, felt like an unwanted guest in the room.

Birdie rose from the bed and moved quietly toward the door. It sounded as if Cheshire sat on the landing, right outside the bedroom. Perhaps he had caught one of the mice Lula insisted scurried around the room at night ever since Wren vacated the space, strangely leaving no evidence of their existence. While the cat refused to cross the threshold, he demanded attention, likely eager to show off his kill.

"Chesh, quiet, you'll wake the whole house," she whispered, opening the door and waiting for her eyes to adjust to the darkness in the windowless landing. She did not want to step on a freshly slain mouse. The thought sent a chilly tremor up her spine.

Cheshire was not on the landing, nor was there any indication of a deceased rodent. But at the bottom of the stairs, she saw his shadow slip by and heard the tinkling of his collar as he turned the corner and escaped her view. *Silly cat*, she thought as she descended the stairs in pursuit.

She took the last step in time to see the cat slink away, down the stairs to the first floor. He was much quicker than his owner and when he made it to the lower level of the house, he let out another yowl, this one more menacing and louder than the one that woke her. She quickened her pace in hopes of catching up to the cat before he woke anyone else. The cat disappeared into the kitchen, where he again let out a cry, this one almost hair-raising.

Birdie entered the kitchen and was taken aback by

the kitchen door standing ajar. Through the open door, the crickets and katydids took over the nightly drone that had been abandoned by the cicadas when the sun ushered the moon into the sky over Stillwater.

There on the back porch, she spotted her cat again and quickly chased after him, eager to nab the feline before he made it to the thick forest beyond the yard. The air was heavy with moisture that felt thick, almost soupy. In the distance lightning flashed, illuminating the heavy clouds. The cat glanced at his owner, then dashed toward the tree line, vanishing into the lush and menacing undergrowth. She dreaded pulling the goat head stickers out of his fur.

"Cheshire, come back," she hissed as she approached the broad woods.

The cat discovered a path leading deeper into the forest, and a thought flashed in her mind: *Where did this path come from?* Grateful the trail would spare her bare feet, she vowed to capture Cheshire before he could move on. She glanced down at the dark passage before setting foot off the soft green grass that was now tended to by a company in town. Roy was far too weak to care for the land that had once brought him such pride. As she looked up, she saw someone walking toward her from down the darkened pathway. Overhead, the clouds parted briefly, allowing the moonlight to fall upon the mysterious figure. It was her sister, Wren. Birdie lost all sight of Cheshire. The temperature of the balmy night plummeted rapidly as if Wren brought with her a cold front.

Birdie reluctantly pushed forward on the once-clear path. She stumbled, her foot kicking something hard, tripping her. She almost landed face-first in the red dirt but caught herself in time. She checked the path again and saw what caused her to trip. It was a rabbit. Not a living rabbit that bolted in front of her. This rabbit was decidedly dead, covered in ice crystals that danced across the poor animal's body when the moonlight fell upon it. A small, gasping scream escaped her lips.

How could anything be frozen in the dead of summer when even nighttime temps barely dipped below triple digits?

She heard a familiar laugh and shifted her focus from the unbelievable frozen bunny to her sister. As she did so, something fell from a tree, hitting her shoulder with a painful thump before it tumbled to the ground, settling at her feet. She took a step back, rubbing her shoulder, and could not believe what she was looking at. A large red cardinal lay motionless on the forest floor. The bird was frozen in a solid block of ice. None of this made sense; her mind couldn't comprehend what was happening. Terror tore through her as she looked up and was confronted with Wren's wrathful countenance; the two sisters so close they could have embraced. But to hold the monster that Wren now was would be baneful. Her sister's face was distorted, the skin taut, giving her red eyes a sunken appearance; bulging veins were etched upon her ashen gray skin. She opened her mouth, and a frigid gale of a silent scream blew through Birdie's hair. Wren lifted her arms and thrust the pink bundle toward Birdie. The forest had grown silent, as if even the nocturnal insects knew to hush their chirping, or they themselves might become shrouded in ice.

Birdie attempted to back away from her sister. She did not want to see what was swaddled in the blanket. Wren only drew closer, again pushing the swaddling into Birdie's face. Birdie stumbled backwards, her bare feet stepping on sticker bushes and stones. The pain was immediate, but she could pay it no mind. She ran into a tree, now trapped between it and Wren. Wren sidled up so her red eyes were staring into Birdie's. Wren's hand, gnarled and gray, lifted a corner of the blanket.

Birdie turned her head and clenched her eyes shut, unwilling to witness the horror Wren forced upon her. But she knew somehow the only way to escape was to give in to Wren's menacing insistence. Reluctantly, she opened her eyes. When she saw what Wren held, terror filled her and escaped in a blood-curdling scream. It was Cheshire, her beloved cat, the one thing that loved her unconditionally without judgment. He was frozen. His mouth opened in a terrified grimace; his eyes wide beneath the icy mask.

She turned to run, needing to escape the sight of her poor cat. She only managed two strides before she tripped again, this time going down, arms splaying. The thing that caused her spill was large and stony and cold. She scrambled to get her feet underneath her again, halting when she saw what had thrown her off-balance. A doe with a full belly, likely pregnant, lay near the path; a sheen of ice glittered as the moon escaped its clouded veil again and shone upon the fallen animal. She clamored over the dead doe and looked toward the farmhouse. It seemed miles away and strewn about the lawn were all manner of forest animals, encased in ice like dreadful lawn statues. She ran, hopping over some and side-stepping others, as fast as she could.

The door seemed to grow further from her, the faster she ran. She tripped over the largest obstacle she had so far encountered. As she pushed herself back up, her eyes fell on the frozen body of her father. From deep in her throat, she raised a helpless scream. "No!"

She wasn't sure if it was the scream that woke her or the ringing telephone.

Chapter Twelve

"Birdie, the hospice nurse says the time is coming. Soon. I need you and the kids here with me. I can't go through your father's passing alone," her mother said tearfully when she called before sunup that summer day.

"We're on our way, Mom," she said, her voice breaking as she tried to fight the wave of tears. "Tell Dad to hang on," she pleaded before hanging up the phone. She didn't give herself time to reflect on the horrifying nightmare and its telling message but was relieved to see her cat curled up in his typical spot at the foot of the bed, alive and well. Now her only thoughts were to get to her parent's home in time to say goodbye to her beloved father.

She went to Iva's room first. It always took at least two attempts to get the girl out of bed.

"Iva, I need you to wake up!" she urged the sleeping child.

Next, she knocked on Marlow's door. The boy rolled over, grimacing and shielding his eyes from the hall light that washed over his face.

"Gram needs us. Get up and get ready, quickly please."

Marlow groaned and stretched but rose and was on his feet when she closed the door behind her. She went back to Iva's room, this time switching on the light.

"I know it's early, but you need to get up. We're going to Gram and Papa's. Let's go." She went to Iva's bed and pulled the covers back. The young girl protested with a groan, yanking the covers up and putting the pillow over her head.

"Get up, now, Iva. Papa needs us." Her tone got Iva's attention, and she sat up.

"Why? What's up?" Iva asked, rubbing her eyes.

"The hospice nurse says the time is near. Papa can't hold out much longer. Gram wants us there. I want us there, to say goodbye." Birdie choked on the words as emotions overcame her. She sat on Iva's bed and pulled her in for a hug. The realization of what this loss would mean to Iva and Marlow hit her like a punch to the gut. They'd suffered so much heartache already in their short lives. Birdie rose to get ready herself. Her eyes flashed by the mirror that hung on Iva's closet door and there stood her sister. She'd grown so used to seeing Wren everywhere, it usually didn't faze her anymore; but today it brought the horrible dream to her mind, and she had to force herself to not be weighed down by the fear and dread the day held for her and her family.

———

Cottonwood fluffs danced on the light breeze, giving the appearance of falling snow as Birdie wound her way across the long bridge that spanned a picturesque pond at the entrance of Camelot Crossing. The sun was just rising, giving way to a spectacular sunrise that didn't fit the grayness of her mood. Iva was in the backseat and had her eyes closed to the beauty outside the car window. Marlow stared intently at his Nintendo DS. Neither of the kids looked when Birdie had to stop and wait for a doe and two fawns to cross Sheffield Court.

When her childhood home came into view, it took Birdie's breath away. The house was stunning. Her father built his bride her dream house, leaving no detail undone. From the perfect shade of pale yellow, the charming turret, and the detailed gingerbread corbels and trim that framed the expansive wraparound porch where crisp white Adirondack rocking chairs sat evenly placed, to the hanging flower pots that Lula lovingly tended, the home was quite a sight, and stood out even in the eclectic neighborhood. Its picture-perfect appearance had been a source of great pride for her father and a monument to the love he had for his family. Birdie had taken its beauty for granted over the years. But today the sight of the home struck her in ways it never had before.

The nostalgic, cheery facade hid the sadness its occupants had faced; and today, its family would be stricken with more grief.

The familiar Karman Legacy Hospice minivan sat in the roundabout. Birdie parked her car behind the van, and the three entered the house through the unlocked front door. Just below the strong aroma of brewing coffee, another scent pushed its way into their senses. It was unfamiliar and organic.

A hospital bed had been set up in Roy's den downstairs, as he had been too frail in his last weeks to climb the stairs to his and Lula's room. The lights were dim and soft music played; Johnny Cash and Kenny Rogers sang Roy's favorite songs.

"Mom, I'm so sorry," Birdie said as she wrapped her arms around the petite woman.

"I know, dear, so am I. The social worker says it might be good to spend a few minutes with Papa alone. Let him hear your voice. Tell him anything you wish to say."

Birdie could tell her mother was on autopilot, not really grasping reality, and was so grateful they had the assistance of care workers to guide them all through the grim process.

Tears poured down Iva's face when she saw her papa. He'd been the only stable male influence in her life. She never had the chance to be a daddy's girl, but she was most definitely Papa's princess. She went to the man and took his hand, as sobs overtook her.

"We'll be in the dining room, Iva." Birdie couldn't hold back the tears; her body trembled with grief. She couldn't believe her dad was leaving them. She fought to control herself, wanting to be strong for her mother.

"Come on, Mom. Let's get you some coffee." Birdie led her mother out of the den.

The social worker and nurse sat at the dining room table, filling out paperwork. The two had been in the presence of so much sadness, so much loss. Birdie wondered how they coped with the emotional toil of the job.

The somber atmosphere was too much for Marlow. He sat in the entryway outside Roy's den and was quickly engrossed in a game on his device.

Iva exited the room in a matter of minutes and rushed to Lula's side.

"Gram, I don't want Papa to die. I'll miss him so much."

"There, there, child. We all will." Lula embraced the girl and began stroking her hair as tears poured down her face.

"Marlow, do you want to sit with Papa for a minute? Say goodbye?" Birdie asked the boy as she knelt in front of him and placed a hand on his knee. He pushed her hand aside, got up without a word, and went to the room where his papa lay.

Marlow left the room a few minutes later. Birdie saw the boy's tense shoulders, and the compulsive squeezing of his shirt in his hands, tell-tale signs he was trying not to cry as he rushed to the powder room and slammed the door.

"Guess it's my turn," Birdie said, rising.

She stood in the doorway of her father's den for a moment, gathering her thoughts and bracing herself to bid farewell to the most important man in her life. When she entered the room, she was taken aback by how he had diminished since the day before. The cancer had wasted him so quickly. His gaunt, skeletal face devastated her. His skin, an off-putting jaundiced gray, stretched over protruding bones. He was unrecognizable. She crossed the room, and took his bony hand in hers, gazing sadly at his mottled and bruised skin.

Shaking off the shock, Birdie sat quietly, listening to her father's labored breathing, contemplating what she wanted to say to the man. How could she possibly sum up a lifetime of love and gratitude in a few moments? It was impossible, but she doubted he could hear. He hadn't been awake for some time now, his pain and awareness muffled by heavy narcotics. Her hope was that he could *feel* her presence, that some part of him knew she was there.

"Daddy, I love you so much."

Nothing from the dwindling figure on the bed.

"You've been the best father, grandfather, better than anyone could have asked for. Thank you for providing us with such wonderful lives."

She couldn't speak anymore; emotions slammed her, and she leaned forward, resting her head on her father's fragile arm. She wondered if there was anything she could tell him to comfort him, to comfort herself. Through his paper-thin skin, she could feel his pulse and believed she could detect it weakening. She stood up and kissed him gently on the forehead before leaning in as if to whisper something in his ear. There was something she wanted desperately to tell him, but she hesitated. What she wanted to say was too awful. She couldn't find the words to use, so she stood upright, preparing to leave when the room was hit with an icy blast of air. The crystal glass in her father's bookshelves rattled in their lead frames. Birdie looked up as the gush of cold air lifted her hair off her shoulders.

In the mirror across the room stood her sister—her face mottled and contorted, her mouth wide open in a silent scream that somehow resonated through the dim room. In her shock and fright, Birdie leaned into her father's ears and whispered the only thing she believed might quiet the furious wave that echoed through the space. She hadn't thought to tell him the truth, Wren's truth, before now. She had held the secret of why her sister abandoned her family to protect them. The reality of it was too ugly, too loathsome. How could her sister toss her family aside for a married man and a bit of money? Birdie believed she had done the right thing all these years. Even as the suppressed dark secret ate away at her own sanity, she held it in so as to not tarnish her family name, to not burden her parents or cause them more self-blame than they already grappled with.

Her father's eyes opened wide, and his frail hand grabbed her wrist with a shocking strength. An indignant glare flashed in the dying man's eyes, at once pleading and accusing. She wrenched her arm free of his hold and whimpered, "I'm so sorry, Daddy!" At that moment, an alarm sounded from one of the machines keeping track of Roy's vitals and the nurse rushed into the room, followed by Lula and Iva. No one outside the den gave a hint they had noticed the disturbance that had just taken place. They were responding only to the jarring beeping of the machines. Roy's eyes slid closed, and he once again seemed unaware of his mournful family as they stood at his bedside.

"You can stay with him. It won't be long," said the nurse as she fidgeted with the tubes and controls on the flashing screens behind Roy's bed. The chirping of the machine slowed, and Roy took a gasping inhale. There was no exhale as the beeping was replaced by a static hum. Roy Clarkson, patriarch of the small family, was gone.

———

Lula broke the silence in the car on the way to the funeral home. "Maybe your sister will show up for the service. We could push it back a little, so she would have time to make it home from wherever she is."

"Don't be absurd, Mom," Birdie said sharply. "Wren

saw an exit lane and she took it. She isn't coming back, not even for Dad."

Birdie was trying so hard to handle her mother with kid gloves, but she was unable to contain her irritation. She glanced at Lula as her mother pulled a tissue from her purse and dabbed her eyes.

Feeling horrible, she tried to backpedal. "Sorry, Mom, I just don't think she will show up. And if she did, what would that do to Iva and Marlow? They don't need that kind of upheaval. Losing their papa is already too much for them to process."

———

Despite Lula's hope, Wren did not show up to lay Roy to rest. From the day that Wren left, until the day of Roy's service, Lula had taken sentinel each morning at the front of the house. When the weather allowed, she would sit in one of the rocking chairs on the wrap-around porch. On days that were too cold or too hot, she sat inside with a view of the long driveway. The morning after Roy's funeral, Lula moved the cozy gossip bench from its place in the window. The street-facing side of the house had never been her favorite spot to take her coffee, but she had always held on to the hope that one day she would see a car pull up and would watch her youngest daughter emerge, having finally decided to come back home. She mustered all her strength and put the chair in the garage.

As she walked back into the house, the silence enveloped her. How would she live in this giant house all alone? What would she do with her time now that she could no longer care for her best friend? She didn't have the answers to those questions, but she made her mind up that she would not spend another minute pining after her missing daughter. If her youngest couldn't swallow her pride to attend the service, she might as well be dead to Lula.

Chapter Thirteen

Every aspect of the children's lives was impacted by their missing mother and the loss of their grandfather. Iva and Marlow acted out their grief in unexpected ways. Their pain often manifested in emotional outbursts and defiance. Birdie felt inadequate and more alone than she ever had. Too concerned with making things right for the children and her mother, she never gave herself the chance to grieve.

Hoping that distracting the children would keep their minds off of their troubles, she enrolled them in every after-school activity imaginable. Iva inherited her mother's flair for the dramatic. She excelled in children's theatre at Town and Gown; but that penchant for dramatics seeped into her everyday life, and the child often threw tantrums and wailed when things didn't go her way. Birdie held some of the blame within herself, convinced she'd done a poor job instilling coping mechanisms.

School officials quickly came to know Marlow on a first-name basis. His dark moods and surly manner found him in trouble at school weekly. Birdie couldn't count the number of times she sat across the desk from teachers or principals defending Marlow and his behavior. Even in her absence, Birdie was left making excuses for her sister. Resentment roiled inside her, but she still managed to carry guilt for this as well. Perhaps she hadn't been affectionate enough with the boy.

Marlow did excel at track, and cross-country was his best event. He ran in a way that made Birdie feel as if he were trying to outrun his problems—like he could leave his anger and sadness far behind him if he just ran fast enough. By the time he was in middle school, he learned to curb his outbursts when his coach threatened to kick him off the team if he got in trouble. This worked wonders for his behavior at school. But at home he became more unruly. Birdie was the recipient of most of his pent-up anger. She tried to have him speak with a counselor, but each time he would clam up and refuse to utter a word. After three such sessions, Birdie gave up.

While she was trying to balance life, caring for the two plaintive youths, her aging mother, and the demands of her career, Birdie realized she was losing her grip on handling life.

The early spring of 2020 brought even more turmoil

for the family, as it did for everyone, as the pandemic began its spread into every corner of the world. Now teens, Iva and Marlow began to test their aunt more and more each day. They were all ill-prepared for being cooped up in the small house, and the tedium quickly took a toll.

Marlow withdrew even further and was unable to focus on learning in the virtual setting. Birdie was relieved that the school was empathetic to children who struggled with online lessons, and he ended the school year with passing grades. The boy was reluctant to leave his bedroom or engage in anything besides video games. Birdie had quickly grown too exhausted, was stretched too thin, to focus on helping her nephew. Her own struggles stymied her ability to render support and guidance to the troubled boy.

Iva grew to be more like her mother with each passing day. She was not one to conform to the limits the pandemic imposed upon her. Birdie found it impossible to keep the girl home. The teen defied her aunt's rules daily, escaping the confines of the house and venturing out to meet up with her friends at the golf course across the street from their neighborhood. Most times Iva would walk right past her aunt, backpack in hand, and take off into the streets; the door slamming on Birdie's words, "Wear a mask! Don't go too far! Be back by sunset!"

Iva never acknowledged Birdie's edicts. Birdie believed that Iva sensed her weakness, her inability to enforce rules, and the teen took advantage of her instability. But Iva did always return home before the sun went down. Birdie took that as a small success and was grateful the girl followed one rule.

Perhaps the greatest challenge Birdie faced in the "new normal" was teaching a class that was not in her immediate presence. On her first day of teaching online, Birdie couldn't find the right Zoom setting. Many of her students logged in late, looking frazzled as they tried to figure out Zoom. Not everyone had their new syllabus, and many had not received emails from the school with the latest assignment sheets. A few didn't have the right books. The chaos of sorting through the details took up the entire hour; and still, nothing seemed resolved. It was more of a lesson in adjusting to a new way of teaching and learning than in quadratic equations. Still, the disorderly shift to virtual learning that nearly every student and teacher struggled with paled compared to Birdie's experience. Wren attended every awkward Zoom lesson held by Professor Clarkson. The unwanted visitor was often the first to check in, occupying one of the squares that filled her computer monitor. Wren's background was always dark. There was no cluttered dorm room, no window where sunlight blocked the student's face, no dimly lit room with a bored student propped up on dozens of pillows; Wren sat surrounded by a shifting blackness. After the first few sessions, most students gave up on cameras and appearances, but Wren never turned the camera off. She wore the same clothes and held the customary pink swaddling in her arms. Birdie's mind felt closer to the edge than ever before.

The majority of Birdie's Algebra students didn't bother to conceal their distractions and disinterest in virtual classes. Wren, however, was seemingly enthralled, only breaking eye contact with the instructor to comfort the bundle in her arms. None of her students ever acknowledged the unfamiliar classmate, and she never participated in classroom discussions, but Wren's appearance threw Birdie off her game—if her bumbling attempts to teach from afar could be considered "game." She stumbled over her own words and answered questions incompletely, or downright incorrectly, as she struggled to maintain her composure while her sister stared back at her from the computer monitor. No matter how many times Birdie kicked Wren out of the meeting and blocked her, she always reappeared within minutes, seemingly unbothered by the rejection. At times Birdie willed herself to contract the virus, simply so she could take a break from the Zoom meetings. She threw caution to the wind, willfully defying the city's mask mandate.

One night Birdie went to the grocery store to collect items for her mother, a habit they had adopted to keep the elderly Clarkson woman away from the dreaded disease. Birdie kept her head down and attempted to do her shopping quickly, aware of the people in masks distancing themselves from her as she passed them in the aisles. But one person stood firmly in Birdie's peripheral line of sight. The person didn't move away from Birdie, but instead walked in front of her cart and stopped. "Oh, sorry," Birdie told the person who had almost collided with her shopping cart. The person didn't move, and when Birdie tried to skirt around them, they shifted to block Birdie's path again.

Now she was irritated and made eye contact with the rude shopper, only to find herself face-to-face with her sister, Wren. Goosebumps rose on Birdie's arms as beads of sweat broke out on her ashen skin. The two women stood close enough to reach out and touch one another, but Birdie withdrew, leaving her cart as a barrier. Now acknowledged, Wren turned and walked away from Birdie; but when she reached the end of the aisle, she turned back and made a summoning motion with her hand. Unable to stop herself, Birdie left her cart in the cereal aisle and followed her sister.

The store was practically empty, as it had been for the past few months as shoppers turned to curbside pick-up to avoid becoming infected. Keeping her distance from Wren, Birdie followed her down the back side of the store aisles. They passed no one else. Wren made a turn and Birdie picked up her pace, not wanting to lose sight of her sister. As Birdie rounded the corner, she ran directly into a man who was surveying the wine selection. Their collision caused him to drop a bottle of sangria. As the bottle shattered, pelting them both with red liquid and shards of glass, she began to apologize.

But the words stuck in her throat when she recognized him. It was the chiropractor, Dr. Hall, the man Euphemia declared as Wren's lover before she disappeared. There was no doubt that it was him. The harsh fluorescent lights caught one of his gold cuff links as he surveyed the mess. The monogram gave the man up—V. H., Victor Hall, Wren's supposed partner in crime.

He wore a mask, concealing most of his face, but she recognized the piercing blue eyes and curly hair that now showed silver at the temples. The man was replying when Birdie caught sight of her sister again, and his words were swallowed up by the ringing in her ears. Her sister stood directly behind Dr. Hall, her face contorted into a silent scream. His head snapped, looking over his shoulder toward the screaming Wren, not seeing her but apparently feeling her presence. Birdie took the chance to duck back around the corner, not wanting to become engaged in any type of conversation with a man who had been close to her sister. She ran back to her cart, grabbed her purse, and bolted from the store, breathless and frightened and confused.

She ran straight to her car, fumbling through her purse to dig up her keys; only to drop them, forcing her to clamor for them on the dark pavement. Once she got to the car, she jumped in but did not start it. She sat, crying, for some time. Just as she regained some sense of composure and got the keys into the ignition, she froze again. Dr. Hall was now leaving the store. As he approached a car, parked directly across from Birdie's, a woman exited the front seat, and Birdie could see two children sitting in the back of the SUV. The woman helped Dr. Hall load the groceries into the back of the vehicle. The man was living his life as if nothing had ever happened.

She'd almost forgotten about him in the nearly ten years that Wren had been gone. Now, she wondered if he was confused by Wren's disappearance; or perhaps, if he had something to do with it. She had always held the belief that he was the man Wren abandoned everything for, and he had been the one who led the supposed embezzling scam. While she didn't know much about the many secrets her sister kept locked away, she never believed Wren to be capable of such a crime.

Birdie sat and watched the two get back in their car and buckle their seat belts. Dr. Hall removed his mask and leaned over to kiss the woman sitting next to him. As she sat, staring, unblinking at the mundane act taking place in front of her, she sensed a change around her. The temperature inside the vehicle dropped. As her she breathed out a puff of vapor air, her eyes slowly tracked from the oblivious couple to her rear-view mirror where she saw Wren, sitting like an unwanted passenger in the backseat. Her sister's head snapped up; and again, she pummeled the space with her terrifying but noiseless scream. Birdie flipped the mirror up, erasing her sister's face but not the chill nor the electric buzz that resonated inside the car. Birdie turned the heater on, hoping to push Wren aside as she followed the Hall family out of the parking lot. She considered trailing them to their next location but talked herself out of it. The entire event left her unnerved. She called her mother and told her she would bring her groceries to her the following night.

"That's fine, dear. Is everything all right?" her mother questioned. "You sound upset."

"Um, no, yeah, everything's fine. I got stuck in my office a bit longer than expected and I need to get home to feed the kids."

"Well, don't worry about me. Nothing I can't make do without until tomorrow. I really wish you'd consider moving out here with me. I'm going a bit stir-crazy all alone out here in this big house, you know. I feel like a prisoner in my own home these days."

"We'll see. I think Iva and Marlow would revolt."

"Nonsense! They'll each have their own rooms here if you don't mind staying in Wren's bedroom like you did when your father was ill. I don't see how sheltering in place would be any different here than it is at your house."

But Birdie knew the children would resist the change, so she tried to placate her mother. "I'll talk to them about it this evening, and I'll see you tomorrow. Have a good night." She disconnected the call before her mother could protest further. While she spoke to her mom, she had been driving on auto-pilot. When she hung up, she realized where she had been heading.

She turned into the vacant parking lot of Parson Chiropractic Clinic. The headlights of her car washed over the sign, which still listed Dr. Victor Hall as a provider. She stared at the sign and grappled with the idea of confronting the man but pushed the notion from her mind. There would be nothing to gain. She remembered Euphemia's words that money had gone missing from the clinic. She wished she knew what had happened. For months after Wren's vanishing act, Birdie had taken to reading the Stillwater NewsPress daily, always scanning for a story regarding embezzled funds at the clinic. What if Euphemia had been lying all along? None of it made sense to Birdie.

It was getting late. She looked at the clock on her dash and couldn't believe she had been sitting in the parking lot for almost an hour, lost in tormenting thoughts. The kids would be hungry, and she had no dinner plan. As she put the car in gear, a person emerged from the shadows of the building. The person moved toward her. Again, it was Wren. Her sister was walking slowly across the parking lot.

She was unable to contain her fear as a terrified scream moved from her chest, releasing into the small space. Incapable of enduring another encounter with her sister, Birdie made the decision to flee. She reversed; and when she righted the car, her sister stood immediately in front of her hood. Intent on leaving as quickly as possible, she couldn't stop in time; her foot weighed too heavily on the gas pedal. A scream built in her throat as she hit her sister. She closed her eyes as the pink bundle Wren held rose into the air from the impact. Her foot found the brake and she slammed it hard. The car came to a screeching halt, and she sat frozen, hands gripping the wheel, eyes clamped tightly. Not waiting for her pulse to slow, she put the car in park, threw open the door, and ran to the front of the car.

There was nothing there.

She fell to her knees and peered under the car, fearing the worst. But again she found nothing. She dared to search her surroundings, hoping no one saw her. The street was quiet, empty. Slowly, she made her way back to the driver's seat where she remained a bit longer, willing her pulse to steady, her breath to calm.

When she felt more composed, she exited the parking lot, turning left. Since she had strayed so far in the opposite direction of home, she decided to get dinner at Nikki's Greek Restaurant, a favorite of Iva and Marlow's. After placing her order and rolling up to the take-out window, images flashed in her mind, and the sound of the shattering wine bottle pulsed in her ears. Nothing made sense.

"Ma'am?"

A concerned voice pulled her from her maddening thoughts.

"Oh, sorry; mind was wandering," she muttered, reaching for the cup holder that held three cups from the young woman at the window. Her eyes fell on the girl's name tag, and she froze, the tray half inside in her car. WREN—the name screamed from the employee's shirt.

Birdie collected herself, realizing the poor girl's reluctance to release the carrier into her trembling hands.

"Your, your name is Wren? Sorry, it caught my eye. It's a rather unusual name."

The girl looked confused. After she handed the drinks to Birdie, she pulled her tag up to look at it.

"No, it's Lauren," she said with an uncomfortable smile.

Birdie looked again and saw the girl's true name. Her mind had twisted the letters and her face flushed red with embarrassment.

"I'm named after some old actress or something. Parents," Lauren said with an exaggerated eye roll. It was obvious to Birdie the girl was doing her best to ease the discomfort of the awkward exchange.

Birdie forced a chuckle.

"Oh, I know. I'm named after a first lady. Parents!"

The young woman glanced behind Birdie's car to the growing line of cars full of people awaiting their order.

Birdie quickly grabbed the bag, thanking the woman. Before she drove away, the woman paused and looked at Birdie. She glanced at the bag, wondering if part of her order was forgotten and waited for Lauren to add another bag or wish her a good evening.

Lauren locked eyes with Birdie and instead of issuing a farewell, she spoke in a cold voice.

"You need to find her, Birdie."

The words echoed in Birdie's ears as she sat unnerved, unable to move.

"Did we forget something, ma'am?" the girl said, a

lighthearted lilt to her voice. It was nothing like the cold words she uttered moments before.

Birdie did not reply. She drove away, leaving the window rolled down in hopes that the brisk night air would return her to her senses.

Once at home, she spread the food out on the kitchen island. Neither child spoke a word to her. They loaded up their plates with dolmas and moussaka and retreated to their rooms.

Birdie made herself a plate and sat in the dining room, alone, nibbling on the food. In the next room, she saw the familiar flashing lights of the television coming on. She called out, "Iva?" There was no reply. She got up and made her way to the family room. Before she could ask if Marlow had turned the television on, she heard the well-known theme music of *As the World Turns*. The spinning globe did not complete its rotation before she snapped the set off. The food sat like a burning lump in her stomach as she retired to her own bedroom, leaving the remains of her dinner sitting on the table.

Chapter Fourteen

2020

Birdie lay in bed, willing herself to sleep. She tried to quiet her mind by focusing on the sound of ocean waves mixed with a calming wind chime tune from an app on her phone. Just as she had managed to stop replaying the scene in the grocery store over and over in her mind and her eyes began to feel heavy, something hit her bedroom window. The light tap drew her out of her lulled state instantly. It sounded like a pebble hitting the glass. Another hit with a louder tap, confirming her suspicions. Wren had often employed this method of tossing pebbles against Birdie's window when they were teens and Wren missed curfew or forgot her house keys.

Birdie hurried to her window and opened the blinds. Her sister stood in the bank of shrubs outside her window. Wren held the pink bundle in one arm and raised the other, pointing to the back of the house; then she turned and faded into the bushes.

On instinct, more than actual understanding, Birdie left her room and tiptoed the few steps to Iva's bedroom. Behind the door she could hear whispering, and she threw the door open without knocking. Iva had one leg out the window. She froze as Birdie turned on the light.

"What are you doing?" Birdie uttered. She crossed the room and grabbed the girl's arm.

"Hey," was all Iva could reply before Birdie spied another figure in the yard.

Birdie yanked hard on Iva and drew her back into the room. Pushing the girl aside, she stuck her head out the window as the person waiting outside for Iva bolted. Iva's backpack lay on the ground below.

Birdie spun the girl around. Outside, they heard the noise of a loud engine revving to life and tires screeching.

"Great! Now he's gone. What are you doing here? Why aren't you asleep?" Iva's face was red with anger. Her resentment had life, like a wave of heat blasting Birdie in the face.

"What am *I* doing here? Who is he, and what are you doing?"

Iva dropped onto her bed. "I don't even know him that well. He was just going to skip town and I decided to go with him."

"Skip town? Go with him? What are you talking about?" Birdie felt like she was admonishing her sister as she had so many times, not her niece. The next words came out of her mouth without thought. "Do you want to end up like your mother?"

Iva looked up, tears streaming down her red face, "It'd be better than ending up like you!" she cried. "At least my mother lived her own life! You don't even have a life; you had to steal hers! You're not my mother and you never will be!"

The words hit Birdie like a punch, knocking the air out of her. She didn't know how to respond but Iva gave her little chance. The girl ran to the bathroom and slammed the door. Birdie could hear her sobs. Marlow opened his bedroom door, rubbing his eyes as Birdie reached the bathroom door.

"What's going on?" he questioned.

"Nothing for you to worry about, Marlow. I'm sorry we woke you. Go back to bed," Birdie told him.

The boy shrugged and returned to his room, closing the door behind him.

Birdie shrunk to the floor in the hallway waiting for Iva to exit the bathroom, wondering what she could say to the girl to make things better. Nothing came to mind. She decided it would be best for them to move out to Camelot Crossing. Not many visitors made their way out to the isolated neighborhood on the outskirts of town.

She got up and went outside to gather Iva's backpack. The pebbles that alerted her to her niece's attempt to run away sat on the ledge outside her bedroom window. She stared at the pebbles. Could her sister be…? No, impossible! She refused to believe Wren was anything more than a figment of her overwrought imagination. The pebbles could have gotten there any number of ways.

Back in the house, Birdie saw that Iva was still in the bathroom, so she went to her own room to pack a bag. Iva's was already packed. She'd help Marlow gather his things in the morning. Birdie did not move from the hallway for the remainder of the night. She nodded off around the time the sun was coming up. When Marlow exited his room around ten o'clock, Birdie informed him they'd be spending the rest of their summer at Gram's house.

She went to the bathroom door, knocked loudly, and said, "Iva, wake up! We're going to move out to Gram's house today. Get yourself ready." She got no reply from Iva but heard the toilet flush and the shower being turned on. Satisfied Iva was preparing herself for the day, she took a suitcase out of the hall closet and went to Marlow's room to help him pack.

As she went about packing Cheshire's belongings, she received a text from a number she didn't recognize.

UNKNOWN: *Better keep an eye on that one. She's more like me than you are willing to admit.*

Heat rose in waves and flushed Birdie's face. Who would send a message like that? Iva herself? Her mystery boyfriend? She made a mental note to call the phone number and check their own records for a number that might match. For now, she felt the walls of her house were closing in on her. She gathered the rest of Cheshire's things and began packing the car.

———

The first night living under Lula's roof, sleep eluded Birdie again. She sat on Wren's old bed awake, wide-eyed, feeling dejected and hopeless. Her despair wasn't soothed by her sleeping arrangements. Once again she took Wren's bedroom. She had hoped to avoid staying in her sister's former space; had even determined a cot in her mother's sewing room would be better. But Lula's sewing room was cluttered now with Roy's belongings. The task of sorting through a lifetime of gatherings was taking her mother far longer than anticipated. At some point, Lula gave up and closed the door to the room; blocking out the insurmountable task of picking through the remnants of her husband's life.

When the kids were too old to share the guest room, Iva chose Birdie's former bedroom as her own, while Marlow took the guest room. That arrangement had never changed, though this time Iva requested her mother's old room. Birdie refused to put the girl in the isolated attic, leaving it the only place for Birdie to sleep. She spent as little time as she could in the bedroom where Wren's essence still clung to life.

She wished she knew how to mend her relationship with the kids and tried her best to convince herself that they were lashing out not so much at her, but at their circumstances. There had been countless news stories about the impact the pandemic was taking on the young. Maybe when the world went back to normal, things would get better. She finally began to doze off with thoughts of happier times, when the difficulties they faced at the moment would be a thing of the past. As she dropped off, she felt the pressure of someone climbing into her bed. For an instant, her drowsy mind convinced her that it was Iva joining her. She came awake, only to hear the subdued snoring sounds that could only be Wren. Birdie turned over quickly to face her bedmate, only to realize she was alone.

"Go away, Wren!" she whispered.

It was a directive to her mind, of course, not her absent sister. But vocalizing her demands did nothing to annul the delusion of her psyche. The small, boxy television that sat in the corner of Wren's attic room since she was young came to life. The volume was set at an ear-splitting level as the spinning globe and familiar intro music of *As the World Turns* blared loudly. Birdie jumped up and ran the few steps to the television, smacking the power button. Before the image and music faded to a blank screen, her bedroom door slammed open. A startled scream escaped her, and a thundering clatter coursed down the hall on the floor below her.

Unable to discern what the noises she heard could be, she rushed out of the room and down the narrow stairway to the second level. The walls of the long hallway held framed family pictures; a history of the Clarkson family beginning with the day Roy and Lula wed all the way up to school photos of Iva and Marlow. Those portraits now shook wildly on the wall. Birdie stood in stunned silence, watching the impossible when the pictures were thrown by an unseen hand. Each frame was hurled across the space one by one, the glass that protected the smiling faces shattering as they crashed against the opposite wall. Another frightened scream escaped her.

All at once, three bedroom doors opened and a hush descended upon the upper level of the farmhouse.

"What on earth is going on out here, Birdie?" Lula broke the silence as she came out of her bedroom, pulling her robe on. A biting gust of air blew through the corridor. Lula's words came out with a puff of vapor.

"Who turned the thermostat down so low? The electric bill's going to be a joke this month," Lula said, still not seeing the mess that lay just beyond the threshold of her bedroom.

"Was it an earthquake?" Marlow asked. His hand searched the wall blindly, before landing on the switch.

As light flooded the dark hallway, the damage shocked them all. Not one frame remained on the walls —the spaces they occupied for years evident by the hooks left protruding in darkened wallpaper squares.

"Who did this?" Lula questioned, her eyes landing on each of them.

"It wasn't me," Iva interjected first.

"Don't look at me," Marlow said, waving his hands.

They all turned their eyes to Birdie at the same time.

"Really? You think I would have done something like this?" Birdie asked. She meant it to be rhetorical, but Iva shifted and looked as if she were going to say something.

"Kids, go on back to bed. Your aunt and I will clean

this mess up. Birdie, get some shoes on and I'll go get some gloves. We'll try to be quiet cleaning this mess up, so you two can get back to sleep."

"I can clean it up, Mom," Birdie offered.

"Nonsense, it shouldn't take long with the two of us on task," Lula said as she descended the stairs to get cleaning supplies and gloves.

Neither Iva nor Marlow had any complaints about being sent back to their rooms.

Birdie knelt on the floor and gingerly removed a photo from the mess of glass. As she held it up to her face, the breath was knocked out of her. The photo was an old one. Birdie and Wren wore matching red gingham dresses and gleaming black Mary Janes with ruffled knee socks as they sat perched in a giant sled next to Santa Claus. Wren flashed an exaggerated smile to highlight that her two front teeth were missing. Birdie's face could not be seen. It had been violently scratched out, her smile obliterated from the photo.

She dropped the picture and crawled to the next picture that lay inside a ruined frame. A piece of glass penetrated her knee as she reached for the picture, but she paid no mind to the pain. This picture as well, her high school senior picture, bore the same scratch marks. Frantically, she grabbed more pictures from their floor, ignoring the shards that cut her legs and hands. A photo of her and Wren—they were older than in the first picture but still young. Between the two sisters was Pistol Pete. Wren's cheeks sported orange and black temporary tattoos, and she wore an excited smile. Birdie's face was gone.

Lula made it back to the second level landing as Birdie clamored over the broken glass, grasping another photo from the ruins. In every picture, Birdie's image had been scratched out as if someone was trying to deny her presence, do away with any image of her.

"Birdie, you're bleeding. What's gotten into you?" Lula exclaimed.

"Look, look at the pictures, Mom," Birdie cried.

"Yes, Birdie. They're the same pictures that have been there forever. Get up! You're making a bigger mess, bleeding all over the floor, child!"

Birdie did rise, not noticing the streams of red that dripped down her legs. She rushed to her mother, stepping on frames, glass, and photos without care.

"No, Mom, look what someone did!" Tears seared her cheeks as she sobbed and held the pictures out for Lula to see.

"I'd say this was caused by an earthquake, darn fracking."

"No, Mom, this wasn't done by an earthquake—"

"Well, I guess you're right. There was nothing out-of-place downstairs. Wouldn't make sense for all the damage to be isolated to the second floor. Not to mention the fact that I didn't feel a thing, just heard a ruckus out here—"

"Mom! Stop," Birdie cried.

"Keep your voice down..." Lula trailed off as Birdie held one of the photos up to her face.

"Well, shoot! The glass must've scratched the picture. What a shame. I've always loved this one. But you know, I've got extras of almost every single one of these. May not be the same size, but we'll be replacing all these frames anyway." Lula rambled on as she began plucking the photos out of the rubble.

Birdie pushed the photos at her mother as Lula stood to straighten the stack she gathered.

"It's not just one; it's all of them!"

Lula inspected the photos, shaking her head. She looked up at her daughter. An expression of disbelief was etched on her face.

"Birdie, why would you do this to your face?" she pleaded.

"No, Mom! I didn't do this," Birdie said. She lowered her voice. "It had to be one of the kids!"

"Nonsense!"

"Well, it wasn't me and I assume it wasn't you. That only leaves two others."

"But why?"

"Because they hate me! They blame me for every-thing when all I've ever done is protected them."

Lula took the photos that Birdie still held from her daughter's hand and placed them on the console table. She wrapped her arms around her daughter, shushing her.

"Now, Birdie, you hush. The kids don't hate you. They're teenagers, and they've been dealt some harsh blows in their short lives."

Lula's words did not comfort Birdie, but she remained in the arms of her mother, realizing how long it had been since she had felt the touch of another person, any person. She allowed herself to soak in the embrace even as a terrifying thought crept into her mind. What if she had indeed been the one to erase herself from the photos?

Chapter Fifteen

The summer of 2020 crept by listlessly, a welcome relief for Birdie. She was glad she didn't have to face her sister in Zoom meetings. Iva and Marlow were grateful to have the craziest school year to date behind them. Lula couldn't be more thrilled to have other people in the house. Even the aging Cheshire boosted her mood with his penchant for chirping at the birds who clamored for seed in one of her mother's many bird feeders. While the cat showed bravado through the window, he ran from the open door. He wasn't much for nature.

A bit of excitement shook up the customarily quiet neighborhood on the fourth of July. It wasn't only the backyard firework displays that lit up the sky that Independence Day; the flashing lights of emergency vehicles descending upon Camelot Crossing caused quite a stir.

"What's with all the hubbub next door?" Birdie asked Lula.

"Guessing someone had a firecracker get out of hand," Lula replied. "If it's a fire, I hope they get it under control quickly."

"It's been so rainy lately, seems like things would be too saturated for a fire to spread."

Birdie stepped outside the front door into the steamy heat of the summer night. She could see bursts of color through the dense forest that separated the new neighbors' house and the Clarkson home. There was no indication of a fire, no smoke in the air, or odor other than the lingering stench of the sulfur and brimstone haze from spent fireworks. She decided she wasn't concerned enough to walk over in the dark. Her mother had met the new neighbors, but she had not and there was the pandemic to consider. Showing up at a stranger's home unannounced would likely be frowned upon.

A few days later, the Clarksons learned it was no simple fourth of July accident that brought emergency vehicles to Camelot Crossing; a body was found on the property next door.

"I got an email from Tim Evens—he's the HOA president—it's ghastly!" Lula made the announcement as she entered the kitchen where Birdie and the teens sat eating breakfast.

"Ghastly? What could possibly be defined as ghastly in this suburban hellhole?" asked Iva.

Without looking up from his phone, Marlow held a hand up.

"Nice one. Put it right here," he quipped.

Iva obliged, smacking her brother's hand from across the table.

"Iva! Language!" Birdie snapped.

Before the teen could finish her eye roll, Lula continued, "They say they've unearthed human remains."

Birdie almost dropped her coffee mug, while Iva and Marlow eyed each other in shock.

Marlow was the first to speak after a lengthy pause. "Could it be, m–mom?" he asked weakly, giving voice to what they were all thinking.

"I can't imagine it would be. Tim said it was found underneath the swimming pool. That pool was there long before Wren left. He suggested I contact the sheriff's department though, just to make sure." A tear slipped down Lula's flushed face, and she brushed it away with a trembling hand.

Birdie went to her mother and led the woman to a chair at the table.

"Mom, don't worry. There's no way it could be Wren. Sit down, I'll make you a cup of tea."

Birdie hoped she sounded confident in her assertion because she wasn't sure she believed it herself. How could a body be found so close to where her sister was known to be before she went missing, and it not be her? Iva had been right about the tranquil suburbia vibe of the neighborhood. The residents of Camelot Crossing weren't the type to be hiding bodies. It seemed surreal.

"I'll call the sheriff right now, Mom," Birdie said as

she set the teacup down. "Please don't get too worked up until we know more of the story."

Birdie went to her father's study, found the number for the Payne County Sheriff, and placed the call. She was transferred numerous times before being connected with a deputy.

"Deputy Ryan Horton, how can I assist you?"

"Yes, Deputy Horton, my name is Birdie Clarkson. We live next door to the house in Camelot Crossing where we understand something unusual has been found."

"Ms. Clarkson, I'm sorry, but I'm not at liberty to discuss any of that."

"Yes, yes, I understand, but my family has particular interest in the findings." Birdie struggled for words, especially since this would be the first time any official would learn of Wren's long absence.

"You see, my younger sister has been missing for quite some time. She was living here at my parents' house when she left. We haven't heard a word from her in years. It just seems like an odd coincidence that the last place she was seen was the house one over from the property where apparently a body has been discovered…"

Birdie's face now felt flushed, her voice shaky as she relayed the story to Deputy Horton.

"You believe she left of her own volition?" the deputy asked.

"Well, yes, we believe so. Several of her personal

items were missing, including her phone and her suitcase."

"Well, ma'am, I can't tell you much, but I don't believe those facts align with what is being investigated at the house next to yours."

"Oh, yeah? Uh, okay, good." Birdie let out an audible sigh of relief. "I mean, not good. She's been gone for almost ten years now, and it's just that my mother, well, she was—" She was rambling now and wished she could end the conversation.

"I understand, Ms. Clarkson. Maybe you should consider filing a missing person case with the police department. I mean, I know it's been nearly a decade since you say your sister left, but that length of time with no communication, especially from someone who has kids—"

"Well, Wren has always been a free spirit … We figured she'd show up when she was ready."

"Even with that likelihood, it'd be advisable to have a case file," he replied, in a brusque tone that sounded judgmental to Birdie. "Could save you from making dozens of calls in these events. That way, if anything were found to match your sister's description, you would be notified."

"Yeah, okay. I'll discuss it with my mother. Thank you for your time, Deputy. You've been very helpful."

"Sure thing, Miss. Have a nice day. And consider filing that report soon."

She lingered in her father's study; its window faced

the property next door. The Clarkson home was deeper in the neighborhood and none of the activity at the house next door was visible, but she could hear the continued commotion that took place one house over. She decided not to share the advice of Deputy Horton regarding filing a missing person report with her mother. Wren was gone, just the way she wanted to be. There was no sense in opening old wounds.

Birdie went to the kitchen and put her arms around her mother.

"The deputy I spoke with is certain the body discovered could not have been Wren's." The tension released from her mother's body in a deflating sigh, and she became heavier in Birdie's arms. Was her mother hoping for some closure, or relieved to hear it wasn't Wren? As she excused herself, she received another text message.

UNKNOWN: *How long do you think it will take before someone finds me?*

She ignored the text, like she always did.

———

The close call stirred more than just memories of the long-missing Clarkson daughter. Combined with the isolation of lockdowns and growing concern over the general state of the country, the season took on a foreboding quality. Birdie could no longer "escape" to the grocery store; even such a mundane chore was too risky while they stayed with her elderly mother. Only grocery pick-ups and the occasional pizza delivery broke the nerve-wracking monotony of the summer.

Of all the inexplicable happenings Birdie had dealt with since her sister's departure, it was the texts that bothered her the most. She continued to receive unwelcome messages from someone who wanted her to believe it was Wren. The messages gradually increased in number until she was receiving two or three per day. Birdie found herself reluctant to look at any text, her hands shaking as she unlocked her phone. She would hold her breath, sometimes dropping the phone as the cryptic texts rattled her. Paranoia crept in with each troubling message. She was coming unhinged and was preoccupied with whom the malevolent messenger could be. Sometimes the messages were so succinct, she believed the sender was watching her. Naturally, Birdie suspected Iva, but she received the texts at times when Iva was in the same room with her. The parental access she had to the girl's phone proved that it wasn't her. Unless, of course, the teen had found some way around Net Nanny. In an effort to put an end to the troubling texts, Birdie confronted her niece.

"Have you been sending texts to my phone from a different phone number than your own?" Birdie questioned Iva, hopeful that her tone came across as casual.

"Why would I send you texts? I'm stuck here with you every hour of the day," the teen replied caustically.

"Then maybe your boyfriend is sending them for

you?" Birdie realized all attempts to sound nonchalant were swallowed up by her paranoid line of questioning.

Iva's mouth dropped open and her face reddened, her eyes set with an incredulous glare.

"Um, no, you put an end to any potential love life I might have had when you chased him off, in your night-gown. I can only hope that it is all forgotten by the time school starts. Besides, I would never give your number to anyone. You already poke around too much in my private life. I know about your stupid spy app. Not cool."

Iva's comments were a slap in the face to Birdie. She tried to maintain her composure, squeezing her fist tightly and taking a deep breath before changing the subject to avoid more nasty comments from the girl.

"Speaking of school starting, I think we should go the virtual route this year, until the virus has run its course. I would feel horrible if one of us got Gram sick."

"Really? To keep Gram safe? Right! I'm sure it has nothing to do with you wanting to keep me under your thumb until I'm like forty. I'm not doing virtual school again."

Marlow walked into the large kitchen and began rummaging through the refrigerator.

"Low, Aunt Birdie wants us to do online school this year!"

Marlow closed the fridge door and, with a carrot stick in his mouth, said, "No way! I am not going to try to go to school from my bedroom again. Sorry, Aunt Bird, not gonna happen."

This conversation wasn't going anything like Birdie had planned.

"You two are being very selfish! I was only suggesting it is the safest option, especially for us to be around Gram!" Birdie's voice grew louder as her anger mounted. Out of the corner of her eye, her sister appeared in the shiny stainless steel of the refrigerator, only enraging her more.

"We're being selfish?" Iva cried. "You've kept us prisoners of this house so you don't have to deal with the outside world! So, what? You want me to flunk my freshman year? Is that it?"

"Of course not, Iva. But, this virus shows no signs of slowing down. The schools will be like petri dishes this year. I want to keep you and your brother, and especially Gram, safe."

Marlow had already vacated the kitchen, apparently believing his statement against online schooling was final.

Lula heard the raised voices and entered the kitchen and immediately began admonishing her daughter. "Birdie, these kids need to be in school. They're young and healthy; it'll be like having a bad cold for them, maybe the flu, if they have any symptoms at all. There's no sense in keeping them home come fall. We'll be careful, everything will be fine."

Birdie was completely outnumbered. "Thanks for your support, Mom," she said.

"Oh, don't get yourself in a tizzy, Bird. All of us need to get out more. I think this virus stuff is all blown out of proportion, anyway." Lula responded, offering no solace to her daughter.

"Mom, didn't you say Roselyn Grant passed away last week? Wasn't she sick with the virus?" Birdie asked.

"Well, yes, but she'd been smoking more than a pack a day since she was younger than Iva and had a laundry list of ailments. She was on her way out before any of this pandemic talk. Rest her soul."

Birdie was defeated. She grabbed a bottle of water from the fridge and left the kitchen without another word. As she did, she got a text notification.

UNKNOWN: *You're losing your grip on things, Birdie-Bird.*

She stuffed her phone into the pocket of her shorts and rolled her eyes as laughter erupted from the kitchen. She wondered how she had grown so distant from Iva and Marlow. Their relationship had deteriorated so badly. Who could have known Wren's pet name for her? It had been years since she had been called Birdie-Bird.

She retreated to the den where she began to scroll through the strange text messages she had received. She'd used Trapcall.com to identify the sender's number, and now it was gnawing on her that it seemed familiar, yet she still couldn't place it. Armed with the new information from her search, she slowly dialed the number. It rang numerous times before someone answered.

"Birdie, it's so cold here."

Birdie jumped and dropped the phone. There was no mistaking it—the voice was Wren's.

With shaking hands, she lifted the phone to her ear again. The person, her sister, had hung up.

From that point on, she made this call numerous times. She even used different phones to call from, and she always got the same response. The call was answered, but only to the sound of howling wind. Her sister's voice never greeted her again. Sometimes she held on the line for long minutes, listening to the familiar sound, transfixed by it almost, waiting for a clue to be dropped. It was hopeless. She didn't think she would ever learn who was behind the unsettling texts.

Chapter Sixteen

Late that summer, someone bought the house that edged the back of the Clarksons' acreage. The home was an unappealing mash-up of glass and cedar, with modern turrets and circular windows. It was also in dire need of updating, as nothing had changed since it was built in the late seventies. The Clarksons didn't know the house had been purchased until the unmistakable sounds of table saws and nail guns disrupted the quiet.

One morning Birdie joined Lula on the back porch before the day got too hot. A fine cloud of fog floated atop the expansive yard. It had always been a peaceful spot to enjoy a morning coffee. The only thing that might disturb the silence was the rattle of the katydids and the chirping of the birds who sought to feast on the noisy bugs. Many mornings, you'd be joined by a herd of deer or a rafter of turkey. But not today. The wildlife drew away from the activity across the wide crevice. The peaceful spot had been taken for granted, and the clamorous intrusion was not appreciated by the animals, nor by Lula.

"Guess I need to find a new spot to enjoy my cup of joe until they're done sprucing up the old Anderson place," she lamented to Birdie.

"The Andersons have lived there forever. I wonder what prompted them to sell at a time like this."

"It was just Pauline living there, ever since her husband passed. I think the place got to be too much for her. Heard she moved in with her son and his family. The isolation was getting to her. I know exactly how that feels. Can't thank you enough for staying out here with your old mom, Bird."

"I'd like to say that my reasons were altruistic, but I did have some ulterior motives. Here's hoping the new family doesn't have any teenage sons," Birdie said, rising from the rocking chair and clinking coffee mugs with Lula. "I've had enough of that racket already, gonna head inside. I've got a mountain of paperwork to get through. My request to teach online in the coming semester was denied. I'm not sure it will be safe for us to stay here with you when we all head back to the classroom, Mom."

"Nonsense," Lula clucked. "We'll get through this fine. This virus can't hang around forever."

Birdie turned back from the kitchen door before opening it. "Let's hope you're right."

———

Lloyd Hilby told his fiancée that he'd found the perfect house. Now he had to prove to her that he was right. He'd gotten the place for a song. Granted, the marigold-colored appliances and burnt orange linoleum were off-putting, but he knew the place would be a gut job when he put in his offer. The sunken bathtub in the owner's suite bathroom kept his mind stirring late into the night, but he was certain with a couple of tons of elbow grease, he could rework the old house into a masterpiece.

"Oh, Lloyd, this place is a mess!" Becky cried upon seeing the home that was tucked into the furthest corner of Camelot Crossing.

So his bride-to-be couldn't envision the place the way he could. He did his best to put her fears aside and focus on the work.

"Just you wait, darlin'. By the time ol' Santie Claus comes to visit, this place will be everything you ever dreamed of," he insisted.

"You're gonna need a Christmas miracle to set this place right."

"Well, maybe December is pushing it. But I think this juice is worth the squeeze and I'm gonna prove it to you."

Lloyd got to work on the interior as soon as he had the keys in his hand. The demolition work had been a breeze. There were plenty of out-of-work helpers eager for wages to make the inside of the house perfect for his

Becky, but his far-fetched deadline loomed in his head, and he realized he vastly underestimated the amount of time the massive project would take.

By December, things were moving along on the inside, so he turned his attention to the grounds. The property was so overgrown with dense brush and trees, he couldn't fathom doing anything else but knocking it all down. He knew Becky wanted a pool and it'd be the best way to keep her three kids out of his hair as much as possible. A pool and maybe a dirt bike trail would be nice. The property was big enough; he'd always dreamed of having a couple of acres to call his own. He just needed it cleared. Lloyd climbed onto the rented bulldozer and began to obliterate the forest as the last of the browned leaves fell, leaving the trees bare.

It took a few days to plow down the dense thicket on the sides of the house. He looked out on the expanse of red dirt he had stirred up. After his first shot at clearing some of the land, it looked more like a martian landscape. But, in his mind's eye, he could visualize the potential the property held, and he decided to push further into the woods behind his house, never once giving thought to the disruption to the wildlife that grazed on the lush greenery and nested in its expansive trees in quiet safety.

He got a bizarre thrill from the cracking and crashing of the old trees, and he continued to push through, forcing out the abundant beauty and life. In his haste, he gave no thought to the environment as he forged his trail through the woods. He didn't consider using the bounty of razed trees for firewood or lumber. He simply continued to devastate the land and push its fallen life into a large decaying pile at the back of the property. It was a time-consuming venture; and on his third day of deforesting, he got his bulldozer stuck in the expansive ravine that separated his property from the farmhouse-style home across from his newly acquired house.

He'd been rolling along on a slight incline near the base of the ravine, enjoying the popping noises the trees made as they surrendered to the giant blade, when the machine started to slide. For a few tense moments, he thought the giant earthmover might just roll over, maybe trapping or crushing him underneath its massive treads. But after the first terrifying jolt, the bulldozer came to rest, dangerously aslant; but thankfully, still upright.

Cursing, he climbed from the cab to see what it was going to take to get the beast of a machine out of the trench. As he walked around to the front of the dozer, he saw his problem. A creek usually ran through the bottom of the gorge, but lack of rain had created a thick mess of sucking red mud and the angle he'd been pushing the machine to climb was too steep. As the dozer fought for grip, its front corner rolled upon an enormous, downed tree trunk. The long-dead oak's wood gave way under the heavy machine revealing a dark cave, while the rear of the dozer found ground on a rocky jut that was so overgrown, he hadn't seen it. He leaned back on one of the muddied grousers and pulled a bandanna from his pocket. As he wiped his face, he contemplated his options for the easiest way out of this predicament. He reached into the cab and grabbed his machete. At the front of the bulldozer, near the previously concealed cavern, he began to whack away at the thick brush and discovered a maze-like tangle of vines and weeds had grown around the snarled roots of the fallen tree. He needed to clear as much of the twisted, decayed debris to see just how bad his situation was—his hope being he could ease the machine down without making things worse. After a couple of swings, the blade of the tool caught on some-thing. He gave the sickle a strong tug and tumbled back when the object gave way and broke from the grip of the thick, embedded web. Righting himself, he saw that he had fished out an old suitcase, the blade of the machete still lodged in the case. He didn't look further into the cavern. For now, the bag had all his attention. He inspected the piece, covered in faded, peeling stickers.

The buckle that held the suitcase together was rusted; the clasp looked as if it were being choked by orange barnacles. He had to work it, but the latch finally surren-dered its contents. His eyes could barely register what he saw. Numerous Ziploc bags holding wads of paper money lay tightly packed within the case. He pulled one of the sealed bags out. Turning it over in his hands, he could see mostly twenties; but also, one or two hundred-dollar bills and several smaller denominations.

A twig popped near his position in the ravine, star-tling him. He swiveled, searching the woods for an approaching person. Seeing no one, he crammed the money back into the suitcase and tucked it under his arm. Holding the case closed, he struggled up the wall of the crevice and made a beeline for the house. Workers standing on stilts and crouched on the floors gave him no notice as he stole away to one of the bathrooms with his recently uncovered treasure, locking the door behind him. He wasn't quite sure why he felt the need to be so sneaky with the find, but he wanted to keep it all to himself, at least until he could figure out where it came from and who it rightly belonged to. The term *finders keepers* echoed through his mind.

He sat on the cold concrete floor with his back pressed against the door, adding another barrier from the prying eyes and curiosity seekers who existed only in his head, as he imagined everyone on site somehow knew of the spoils contained in the suitcase. He opened the deteriorating luggage and first started counting the baggies. Commotion and voices just outside the bathroom door alarmed him, and he called out, "Occupied! Give me a few." No one responded, but he felt too on-edge in the house with so many others. He closed the suitcase, tucked it under his arm again and made his way out the front door, rummaging in his front pocket for his keys. His truck was a mess. He searched a few minutes behind the seat and came up with an old hoodie. He placed the suitcase on the floorboard of the passenger side and covered it with the old jacket. Eyeballing his concealment, he felt certain no one would be able to make out the suitcase, even if they peered directly into the windows. As he walked back to the house, he'd forgotten all about the stranded bulldozer. Instead, he was consumed with the gnawing question: How much money had he stumbled upon? And should he keep it a secret from Becky?

He made every effort to appear casual, making out as if he was inspecting the day's work, but nervous sweat beaded on his brow, and he couldn't shake the feeling that the day workers were looking at him sideways. He saw two men heading up the walk, back from a smoke break or who knows what. As he watched the men approach, he was certain they paused and glanced at his truck. His paranoia got the best of him, and he decided to call it a day.

"Taking off for the day," he hollered to men in the hollowed-out house. "If you're the last one out, be sure to lock the door and flip the outside light on."

Lloyd did not wait for replies. He rushed to his truck and took off down the tranquil, oddly named lanes of Camelot Crossing.

He followed the familiar route by muscle memory, oblivious to anything but his erratic thoughts about his newfound windfall. His mind and body didn't register the shift from the roughly paved Range Road to the dried-out country road and its overgrown weeds, powdered a ghostly white by the gravel dust kicked up from countless tires. The pale overgrowth reached out and brushed his truck and pebbles pinged off the undercarriage as he sped home over the heavily pitted, gravel road. He rolled through every stop sign, pausing only for the dust cloud that engulfed his truck to subside enough to make sure he wasn't being followed.

At first, Lloyd was too caught up in his paranoia to see the figure that sat in the rusty bed of his ancient Dodge. She was easy to miss and wasn't bothered by the rough terrain, nor by the suffocating brume of grit. But as he pitched up to the last stop sign before his turn onto the rural route where his home rested among a tight row of identical low-slung tract houses, he saw her in the rearview mirror. A girlish scream escaped his throat.

Frightened, he jerked the wheel. The truck jumped into the runoff ditch outside his makeshift neighborhood. When the pickup came to a jarring stop, he turned to look, knowing it was impossible, but hoping that his strange passenger had not been thrown. She remained in the bed but scurried toward him at an impossible speed. Her face was separated from his by only the grimy slider window that separated the cab from the bed. It was then he saw her clearly—the blue lips and red eyes and the map of purple veins that twisted beneath her gray skin. Her mouth hung open in a silent scream that fogged the glass. Terror and instinct forced him to clamp his eyes shut as the truck shook violently. As suddenly as the shaking began, it stopped, and he dared to open his eyes. The woman was gone as if she had dissipated along with the plume of road haze.

Anxiously, he groped for the old jacket. A lump of fear built in his chest. What if he'd imagined the case full of cash, just as he had dreamed up a woman riding in the back of his Ram?

"Whew," he gasped, realizing the case was still there. After he caught his breath and his pulse slowed, he threw the truck into reverse, and it bucked back onto the road. He took a sweeping glance around him, hoping none of the neighborhood kids and dog walkers had spotted his suspicious actions. It'd been so long since kids were in school, it seemed there was always a gaggle of them roaming the back county roads. He was relieved to see no one was out this afternoon.

For the remainder of the short drive, Lloyd had to force himself to take deep, calming inhales and long, drawn out exhales. While he wouldn't last two minutes before he spilled the news of the suitcase full of money to Becky, he'd never speak of the woman in the back of his truck, even as she haunted his nightmares for years to come.

Becky sensed something was up before he made it all the way into the house. As he took off his dirt-caked boots just inside the door, she spied him from her vantage point at the kitchen sink. She dried her hand with a nearby paper towel and reached over to pause the country music blasting from her phone before returning to slicing onions.

"What are you doing home so early? You aren't sick, are you? Did you forget something?" It was more of an interrogation than curiosity. "The kids aren't even back here begging for an afternoon snack yet."

He silently cursed himself for the obvious timing blunder and stole a glance at the clock on the microwave. On a normal day, he wouldn't arrive home for another three or four hours.

"Becky, I'm gonna need you to sit down."

"Sit down? Nonsense! I'm prepping for supper. If I don't get this done now, it'll be a bowl of Frosted Flakes for everyone. I can't get a dang thing in the can when the kids get back from terrorizing the neighborhood. Lord, I need them to open the schools back up. None of 'em are gonna learn a thing this year."

Lloyd approached Becky and took the paring knife from her hand. It looked like she was prepping for fajitas, one of his favorite dishes, but the chopping of onions and peppers would have to wait.

"Beck, this is important. Drop what you're doing and take a seat over there," he said in a cheery voice, so as to not anger his hot-headed future wife. "It'll be worth it, you gotta trust me. Have a seat and I'll be right back."

He anticipated her putting up more of a fight than she did and congratulated himself on getting this far without her flying off the handle.

He ran to the garage and retrieved the suitcase from his truck. Back inside, Becky was checking her fingernails and shaking her crossed leg vigorously to make sure he knew how put out she was.

"Okay, hon, try to keep it together when you see what I found today," he told her as he approached her. He set the worn luggage on the faded and cracked tabletop, and she shot him a look that left little doubt that she was perturbed.

"Lloyd Michael Hilby III," she exclaimed. "You pulled me away from what I was doing to show me a dirty, old suitcase? I'm not cleaning that mess up. Why'd you have to put it up here anyway? Get that filthy thing off my table! The nerve—"

Her tirade was silenced, and her eyes widened as Lloyd opened the trunk. She didn't seem to notice the clumps red dirt that fell from the table onto the floor as he did so. He looked to Becky and back to the money several times as she sat staring in silence.

"Lloyd, what? Where? Is it real?" she stammered, finally breaking the peace. "Can I touch it?" she asked as her hands already snatched up one of the bundles that had been spared the elements by the large plastic bag.

"I found it on the property, our property," he told her. "I'm pretty sure that makes it ours."

"Where on our property? Was it hidden in a wall? Is there a crawlspace you didn't know about?" Becky was questioning him while rifling through bag after bag of what appeared to be varied denominations.

"Uh-uh, no, it was in the ravine."

Becky dropped the money and fixed him with a wary look, one that Lloyd had become very familiar with. A look that warned him her wrath was fixing to be let loose on him. He braced himself as Becky swatted his arm. The smack didn't hurt, but he knew she was building up steam.

"The ravine? The ravine, you say?" She hadn't raised her voice, but her words blasted him in the face. "What makes you think the ravine is our property? Have you never heard of an easement? How sure are you that the ravine is even part of our property? You have it assessed yet, like I told you to?"

Lloyd flinched as she used exaggerated finger quotes to punctuate the words, "the ravine."

"Well, now, no. I'm not a hundred percent on that fact…" he started.

"Not a hundred percent?" The finger quotes had returned, and Lloyd flinched each time she used them, expecting a hand to lash out at him again.

"I'm not sure you've been a hundred percent of anything since the day you were born!"

"Now, Becky, that's not necessary."

She stood up, pacing the small kitchen now, hands on her hips. Abruptly, she turned back toward him, and he shrunk away from her.

"Who knows about this find of yours?"

"No one! Well, 'cept you now. We're the only ones who know."

"How can you be sure of that?" she pounced back. "What if someone saw you? Heck, you have half the town's unemployed out there right now, trying to turn that eyesore into a dream house." Again, with the finger quotes. "What if one of them saw you?"

"No, I swear. I was in the ravine alone. I got the dozer stuck." He paused, waiting for her to ridicule him.

She said nothing. Just stood tapping her toe, eyes fixed on his reddening face.

"When I tried to clear it, my machete hit this, this…" He motioned his hands at the suitcase.

"Go on," she replied.

"I grabbed it up and ran inside the house; locked myself in the bathroom to catch my breath. Then I put it in the truck and left. I didn't want anyone else to spot it."

She was pacing again, and he could see the wheels turning in her mind. He sat quietly, motionless, waiting for her to say something.

"Well, if you're sure no one saw you…"

"I'm pretty sure of that. There wasn't anyone else out there. None that I could see anyway," he responded eagerly.

"You say it was in the ravine? What else was out there?"

"Whole lotta nothing: fallen trees, vines, brambles, undergrowth, the usual."

"So, you didn't look around for a person it might belong to? Any more suitcases? I swear, Lloyd."

"Now listen, I was as stunned as you are now, seeing a suitcase full of money. I don't know what you're expecting out of me, but—"

"You're right, you're right, calm yourself on down, hon." She was speaking softly to him and started rubbing his shoulders. "Was there anything else in there besides the money? Any identification? Clues to say who left it there?"

Her kneading hands started to melt away the tension that built in the past frenzied hours, and he relaxed a bit for the first time since he'd spotted the stash.

"Just an old phone charger. It's still in there."

"I'm thinking we should head on back down there, check things out, take a closer look," she said in her thinking-out-loud voice.

"I was gonna call Cowboy Towing and have 'em come haul that dozer out."

"Yeah, no, we'll have to wait on that, at least 'til we've had a chance to poke around out there a bit more. Sun-up tomorrow's when we'll do it; before the kids get up. Maybe there's more suitcases out there. Just maybe. For now, go put that thing in the top of our closet."

He moved to gather up the case and the treasure it held.

"Be sure to wrap it up in a trash bag first. I don't need that mess all over the closet too," she told him before she made her way back to the sink, washed her hands, and started cutting bell peppers.

Chapter Seventeen

Birdie stood in the kitchen, staring out at the ruined earth across the divide. Spindly trees stripped of their leaves draped grim shadows over the red, barren wasteland. She spotted something moving through the gray woods. It wasn't until the object breached the skeletal tree line that she saw it was her sister Wren. For a moment Birdie believed the vision to be solid and true; her sister had finally returned home. With shaky hands, she put her coffee cup down on the counter nearby. The mug barely made safe contact with the well-worn butcher block as she couldn't take her eyes off Wren. Mesmerized, she leaned in; silently willing her sister to come closer, while resisting the urge to run out to greet her.

Wren didn't move past the edge of the tree line. Instead, she stopped to check the bundle in her arms, the mysterious swaddling she held in Birdie's troubled visions. Birdie nearly jumped out of her skin when, behind her, a hacking cough broke the silence. In that instant, Wren disappeared again; not receding into the forest, but simply evaporating from view.

"Sorry, didn't mean to scare you like that," Lula told her daughter.

As she turned away from the window, she saw Wren again—this time standing behind her mother. Before Birdie had time to register what she was seeing, Wren's head snapped up, and she blasted the room with a silent scream.

"Did you feel that?" Lula asked Birdie. "Felt like a tremor." Aside from Victor Hall in the grocery store months ago, this was the only other time since Wren vanished that someone besides herself took notice of the illusory woman's wrath. This awareness shocked Birdie more than any of the visions of her sister.

"Oh well, probably that blasted new neighbor and his deforesting project," Lula said distractedly as she shuffled to the medicine cabinet in the kitchen.

"Are you all right, Mom?" Birdie questioned.

"Got a little tickle in my throat and feeling a bit chilled," her mother replied as she rifled through the medicine cabinet. "It's too quiet down here. Shouldn't the kids be in the study with their schoolwork?"

"First day of winter break. I thought I'd be nice and let them sleep in." Birdie retrieved her coffee mug and took it to the pot for a refill.

"They haven't been in a classroom since before Thanksgiving. Seems like the school year hasn't been grueling enough to warrant sleep-ins. I don't know why they even bother with this distance learning hogwash. Kids belong in school," Lula fumed, inspecting a box of cold tabs.

"I should have known they'd be yanked back-and-forth with quarantines and exposures. I wonder if they will be going back to in-person at all this year."

"Nonsense! It'll work its way through like any bug and die down soon. They'll be good to go after the holidays."

"You're much more optimistic than I am, Mom."

Their conversation was interrupted by Iva, who came into the kitchen rubbing her temples. The teen was still wearing her pajamas.

"Gram, I don't feel good. Do you think I've got a fever? I'm burning up but shivering too."

The girl's color was off. She got near Lula and bent down, accepting the old woman's cold hand on her forehead.

"Oh my, Birdie, this child is burning up. Take a seat here before you fall over," Lula told Iva as she pulled a seat out at the old kitchen table.

"I've never felt worse in my life. Do you think I have the virus?"

"Not sure about that, but you've got something. Let me get you some cold medicine and Tylenol. Birdie, grab some orange juice from the fridge in the garage, would ya?"

Lula was doling out large capsules to Iva when Birdie

returned with the orange juice. She poured a small glass of the cold drink and handed it to Iva. The girl took the pills and the juice and gulped them down.

"Ugh, that burns, and I think that juice is bad. It doesn't have any taste," Iva complained.

Birdie and Lula shared a knowing glance before Lula doubled over in a coughing fit.

"Well, it looks like I will be Aunt Nurse for a while. Both of you, get back to bed. I'll get some soup started and check on Marlow."

Birdie found her nephew shivering under his blankets and took his temperature. It registered 102.

"I'll bring you some medicine and orange juice. I guess our house is a quarantine zone now. Once I get you all settled, I'll put in a call to the doctor."

Marlow moaned a reply and pulled the blankets tighter around his face.

In one of the mysteries of the pandemic that held the entire country in its grips for months, Birdie herself never felt more than slight congestion and a bit of a foggy mind; more like allergies than the feared virus. Her health made it possible for her to coddle her wards and her mother. For several days, she was pulled in many directions. Each of her patients required individual attention as their symptoms varied. After about two weeks, the sickness was a thing of the past for the hardy teens. But Lula was hit harder than her grandchildren. Birdie worried that she wasn't able to provide the care her mother needed. As her condition worsened, Lula started telling Birdie things that shook the frazzled woman to her core.

"Would you mind helping an old woman change her night clothes?" Lula asked one morning when Birdie arrived to check on her. "Must've broken a fever while I slept. I'm drenched and so uncomfortable." Lula struggled to sit upright and fought with her blankets. Birdie did not like her mother's pallor, and she detected a blueish tint to the older woman's lips and fingernails.

"Of course, Mom. Hold still. Let me help you. If you can make it into your chair, I'll change the sheets."

"That'd be a dream, Birds. Thank you, dear," Lula whispered.

After situating her mother in the chair by the bed, she gently tugged her mother's robe up around her neck and covered her lap with a blanket; then began the task of changing the sheets. It took Lula several minutes to catch her breath from the minimal effort she exerted. Once she could speak, she told Birdie, "I spoke with your sister last night."

Lula paused, arms in the air as the flat sheet fluttered to the bed.

"Mom, that's not possible. Wren isn't here," she said in a pacifying tone.

"She's visited me a few times since I took ill, but this was the first time she talked to me," Lula pressed on, ignoring her daughter's comments.

"How about we get you into the washroom and

freshen you up a bit?" Birdie replied, dismissing her mother's claim.

Lula couldn't speak for some time. She was too winded by the mere act of using the toilet and getting a quick sponge bath. She made Birdie stop on the short walk back to her bed, saying, "My lungs burn." Birdie could tell the effort to breathe left her mother drained.

As Birdie helped her mother settle back into the bed, Lula grabbed her daughter's hand with surprising strength. Her eyes pleaded with Birdie to stay instead of making a quick exit. Birdie waited patiently until her mother was able to speak again.

"She … she told me—" Lula started. Her body was wracked with a coughing spell, leaving her unable to finish her thought.

Birdie rose from her mother's bedside and made her way to the door. "That's it. I'm calling Dr. Sawyer."

"She said you have something to tell me." Lula closed her eyes upon uttering the sentence.

Birdie crossed her arms and frowned at her mother before addressing her.

"Oh really? So your daughter, who has been missing going on ten years now, just sauntered into your room last night and said that I, *I* had something to tell *you*?" Birdie couldn't hide her anger, nor her alarm, and fought to regain her cool.

"Sorry, sorry, Mom. You need your rest. I'll be back in a couple of hours with more medicine and some soup."

"Don't bother. I can't taste it and I'm not even hungry. And don't bother the doctor with this either."

Birdie took a beat to quiet her emotions. "You need to eat to help you get your strength back. But for now —rest."

Birdie made a swift exit, eager to end the uncomfortable conversation.

She busied herself in the kitchen, washing dishes and disinfecting every surface she thought the crippling virus might be lingering on. It was too late, of course; it had burned through the Clarkson home already. But it was the only thing she could think to do.

After cleaning, she checked on Iva and Marlow. While the teens were feeling much better, they still suffered from a persistent fatigue. The two lay in their beds, their faces lit up by their phones. They each barely gave a grunt when she asked how they were doing.

"I made a pot of soup. Make sure you eat soon," she told the teens before making her way to her mother's room.

Birdie entered the dark room without knocking. Her mother's breathing sounded labored and had taken on an unsettling rattle.

"Mom, I really think I should take you to the ER. You aren't getting any better. You've been practically bedridden for weeks!"

"Nonsense!" Lula croaked. "I'm not going to die all alone with a tube shoved down my throat, Birdie! Or worse yet, give up the ghost in the hallway of an overcrowded hospital. I mean it. I've seen the reports on the news. If you take me to the hospital, you might as well take me to the funeral home."

The burst of indignation left Lula depleted. She struggled to sit upright to drive her point home; and before speaking the last words, she collapsed back onto the pillows Birdie had stacked behind her in an effort to keep her mom from lying prone.

"Okay, Mom, relax. I won't take you if you don't want to go, but they have treatments there that might help. It's really hard to watch you suffer like this. Calm down, please. Don't get so worked up."

Helplessness washed over Birdie. Lula grabbed her arm weakly as she turned to leave the bedside. Helplessness turned to cold dread with Lula's next words.

"I talked to your dad last night, too," Lula whispered.

Her mother was now delusional, having fever dreams, something.

"Mom, please stop!" Birdie attempted to protest, but after a long pause, Lula continued. The sound of the older woman's breathing frightened Birdie, almost as much as the next thing her mother said.

"I won't stop because it is true. He told me that—" She didn't finish the sentence as a wave of unproductive, barking coughs took over. It did nothing but sap more of the fragile woman's energy.

Birdie stood helplessly by. She had done everything she could think of to ease her mother's symptoms. The humidifier hummed softly as it blew a cloud of heated water vapor. She faithfully refilled the tank and cleaned the filter, but it seemed to do no good. Birdie pushed fluids and medicines on her mother routinely, and most times wouldn't take no for an answer, but she could see her mother fading. If only she would go to the hospital. Birdie felt the weight of her mother's feeble existence pushing her down even further.

"He told me I wouldn't survive this," Lula finally managed to utter.

The words took Birdie by surprise, and she sat next to her mother, shaking her head numbly, unable to find words.

"He told me to stay here, in our home. Said he'd be coming for me soon."

Birdie was shaken to the core but had no reply for her mother. She hadn't noticed the woman had grabbed her hand while she spoke. Her grip was tight, and she did not let go; so Birdie stayed, remaining silent. She was envious of her mother's faith. Her certainty that she could be reunited with her husband. Desperation engulfed her.

Birdie believed her mother had fallen back into a fitful sleep and let out a startled whimper when her mother spoke again.

"Your sister has been here too. She talks to me."

This admission broke Birdie's stupefied silence.

"Okay, Mom, that's enough! I don't believe that Wren is sneaking into your room for daily heart-to-hearts." Birdie wrenched her arm out of her mother's grasp and rose. "You need to rest now. I'll be back with some soup and juice in a bit." Birdie made her way across the dark room to the door, but her mother wasn't finished speaking.

"She said to tell me, Birdie. Her voice is getting louder. I'm running out of time."

A chill took over the room and Birdie saw herself in the mirror above the antique dresser. Wren stood behind her, a silent scream on her face. Birdie turned to her mother, more to focus on something other than her visions of Wren than anything. Lula had fallen asleep, her breathing raspy and choking. Sweat dripped from Lula's face, her silver hair lay in damp tangles on her pillow. Birdie feared this was the last time she might speak with her mother and, while she knew she should stay—hold her mother's hand, rest a cool washcloth on her fevered brow—she ran.

The door stood open—but as she approached it, it abruptly slammed in her face. She grabbed the knob and flinched; it was icy cold, burning her fingers, and did not give. There was no fight left in her. She slumped to the floor, sobbing. Her phone notified her of a text from the unknown number,

UNKNOWN: *She's right, you know. Time is running out.*

She tossed the phone down on the faded rag rug and whispered, "Tell her what? I don't know what you want."

She heard a soft knock on the door. "Aunt Birdie, are you in there?"

It was Iva. The girl's voice shook her from her despair

and brought her back to the moment. Birdie stood, and this time the door opened with ease.

Iva saw her aunt's red eyes, as Birdie did her best to wipe her own tears away.

"What's wrong? Is it Gram?" the girl said, pushing past her.

"No, no, she's sleeping. She refuses to go to the hospital and I—"

"She doesn't need the hospital. She'll be fine. I'm much better and Marlow is over it already. She just needs a bit more time. Gram is strong. Stop stressing out so much."

Birdie had no response to her niece's optimistic outlook. She believed it would be best to let the girl believe in the possibility of a turnaround in Lula's health.

"There's something going on in the woods. It's like déjà vu from this summer," Iva said, changing the subject.

"What? What are talking about?" Birdie asked.

"I heard some ATVs or something back there. When I looked out my window, I saw a bunch of people searching the forest.

Chapter Eighteen

Sun-up was still a couple of hours away when Lloyd and Becky set out in hopes of finding more suitcases full of cash. Becky was a bit fretful that one of the kids might wake up and discover their absence.

"Yeah right, Beck. Those kids don't wake up till you've hollered at them three times or more. They ain't waking up early for nothing," Lloyd said to quiet her concerns.

"You're right. You got the flashlights?"

"Yes, hon,"

"They got fresh batteries?"

It was always something with his fiancée. He wondered how she kept all these details in her head like she did. "Well, I don't think they're fresh, but they're bound to have enough juice in them for this."

"Lloyd, if we get out there and these lights don't

work…" She trailed off, but Lloyd got the gist and said a silent prayer that the flashlights remained lit.

"Couldn't have picked a colder morning for this, could you?"

Lloyd saw the look on Becky's face and decided not to reply. He'd kept his truck parked in the garage last night and was grateful for that. When he backed out of the drive, he saw that Becky's car was shrouded in a layer of frost. If he had to clear the windows before they left, he would have lost precious time, and he would have had to listen to Becky's nitpicking even longer, especially since he had no clue where he'd put the window scraper.

Most of the residents of Camelot Crossing were still asleep as Lloyd and Becky made their way to the back of the neighborhood where their home sat. The only living thing they encountered was a fox. The animal's breath left clouds of vapor trailing behind him as he scurried across the road. The headlights of Lloyd's truck reflected on the frost that clung to the leaves and grass, making the neighborhood look as if it was blanketed in twinkling stars.

All was quiet at their land as well. The workers wouldn't be showing up for at least two hours. Lloyd parked in the driveway that was strewn with construction materials and killed the engine, throwing them into darkness.

"I forgot my dang gloves," Becky complained. "You got an extra pair in here?" She was rummaging through the glove box.

"I don't think so," Lloyd replied. "Here, you can use mine."

"Well, let's do this," Becky said, putting his gloves on. Her small hand was dwarfed inside them. "Way I see it, this could be better than winning the lottery."

"How you figure?"

"Well, no one has to know about this windfall. Won't be any greedy family around sniffing for handouts. Won't have to hand half of it over to the government either."

Lloyd had learned not to question Becky's musings. He went around to her side of the truck to help her down, and she followed him to the spot where he'd found the suitcase, the search made easier by the hulking bulldozer.

"Good grief, Lloyd, you had to knock down everything? This looks horrible in the dark. Can't imagine how ugly it is in the daylight. How long you figure it'll take for things to grow back?"

"There's a crevice right down here. It's where I found the case," Lloyd said, ignoring her questions.

A countless murder of crows, disturbed by the pair, took flight from their roosts. Becky let out a quiet gasp, and Lloyd shrunk away from the trees that towered over them. The sky became darker as the birds rose. Their noise stirred other animals nearby.

Becky slapped at Lloyd, silently admonishing his foolishness.

"It was right here," he whispered as he shone the beam of light into the knotted thicket.

"Can you see anything else in there?"

"Yep, there is something else. I can't reach it from here."

"Well, get your machete and start swinging."

Instantly Lloyd realized he'd made a terrible mistake; one that he'd be hearing about for days. He'd left his machete in his truck.

"Yeah, um, gotta run back to the truck to get it. Wait right here," he said casually, hoping his carefree tone would cover the blunder.

"You kidding me? We came all the way down here and you don't have your tools? I swear to Pete, you'd leave your head behind if it weren't attached. Not that that head is full of anything but air—"

Lloyd was already scrambling back up the hill to his truck. Once he got there, he grabbed an ax as well. He had the sense to realize he'd need more than a machete to break through the knotty mess, no matter what Becky thought. He spied a pair of work gloves and grabbed those too. They weren't as good as the pair he'd lent to Becky, but his fingers were already numb, and he knew they'd be useless uncovered.

He found Becky pacing and jumping up and down a bit in the clearing he'd created.

"I think the temperature's dropped since we got out here," she fussed.

"Come down here and hold these flashlights for me, so I can see what I'm doing."

Lloyd handed her the flashlight he carried, and she

took position far enough back from him so that she wouldn't get whacked, but close enough to flood the area with light.

"This ridge is so overgrown, not even the smallest critter could've made its way in here to make a home," he grunted as he hacked away at the overgrowth. After several minutes, he'd cleared enough to get a better look at the small cave.

"Oh, Becky, I see something in there," he said excitedly.

"What is it? Another suitcase?"

"Nah, looks like a boot, a snow boot, maybe. I think I can reach it."

The boot broke free of its thorny confines with a force that threw Lloyd back several feet. He fell into the frosty brush, landing dangerously close to the blade of the ax. Becky paid no mind to the potential that Lloyd might have been injured by the fall as she hurriedly tucked the flashlights under her arms and snatched the boot out of his hand. The contents of the shoe remained stuck inside as she wrenched it away from him. She peered inside it. Lloyd could almost see the dollar signs in her wide brown eyes as she tipped the boot into her free hand and shook it sharply. Her eyes widened as the gray shards fell upon her open hand then tumbled to the ground. She flung the boot across the forest floor with a scream; then stumbled and fell as she tried to run.

"What is it? What's in there, Beck?" he asked as he offered a hand to help her up.

"Oh, my God, Lloyd! How'd you talk me into this?" she whispered. She was rubbing her gloved hands on the back of his coat, eager to free herself of any remnants of the objects she had just held.

"I'm no doctor, but I think those are bones, Lloyd. Bones from a person's foot!" She was backing away from him now, averting her eyes from the boot; her arms wrapped tightly around herself as if she could shield herself from the find.

"Nah, that's crazy. How'd you even know what foot bones look like?" Lloyd was certain the usually level-headed woman was overreacting.

"Looks like bones, and they're in a shoe … one plus one," she replied, the shock leaving her voice to allow for another dressing-down.

"No way we're ever going to find whatever they were now," Lloyd said as he picked up one of the flashlights from the leaf-covered ground and ran the beam over the place Becky stood. She looked dumbfounded, a rare expression for her, as she visibly trembled.

"Lloyd, we need to get out of here," Becky said as she began stumbling back up the rocky embankment.

"Don't you leave me alone down here!"

Lloyd gathered the ax, machete, and other flashlight as he tried to figure out how he was going to get back up the sharp incline with his hands full of sharp objects.

"Becky!" he whisper-shouted, "get back here and help me out."

It was no use; Becky had made it halfway back to the truck, and she wasn't turning around.

He tucked the flashlights inside his coat and slowly made his way back to the truck. The sun was just peeking over the clouds as he put the tools in the back of his truck. Inside the cab, Becky was rocking back and forth. He didn't know if she was trying to warm herself up or calm herself down, maybe both.

"Woman, you need to settle down. Now I know your mind might play some tricks on you if you find an empty boot full of pebbles or whatnot—"

"Lloyd, those were no pebbles! I'm telling you; they were bones. Something's bad wrong here."

"Well, what do you suggest we do now? I don't think anyone saw us, but we left that boot there; we left everything exposed down there; and we still have the problem of the bulldozer being stuck. I rented that thing, can't just leave it down there and hope that no one ever notices it."

"I know. I know, I need some time to think." Becky had a focused glare in her eyes and Lloyd could tell her mind was wrangling with how to handle their discovery.

"We don't know what we may have stumbled on, Lloyd. A suitcase full of cash; now a boot full of bones. Did you see anything else in there?"

"Now that you mention it, yes, I did. There was another boot and what looked to be some clothes."

"Oh, Lord, I wish you hadn't said that. Lloyd, what if there's a body in there?"

"Crazy talk! One body found in a neighborhood, even one as odd as this one, is enough for one year."

"Pretty sure that's not how things work, Lloyd. The sun's coming up. You need to call all your contractors and cancel work here today."

"Nope! I've got a schedule to keep and none of those men are going to take kindly to losing a day of work. Most of them are probably already on their way out here anyway."

"You're probably right. We need to get back home. Hurry up, we can't be seen out here."

"Cool your jets, Becky. We have every right to be here on our own property whenever we so choose."

Becky didn't speak as they made their way back home. The kids were, as expected, all still sawing logs in their beds. Becky needed Lloyd's help to make a pot of coffee. She was no longer chilled from the icy morning, but her hands were still shaking beyond her control.

"I've got to come up with a plan to get us out of this," Becky said, accepting a steaming mug from Lloyd.

"I say we ignore it. I'll go tuck things back inside that outcropping, have Cowboy Towing get the dozer out for me, and go about our lives, business as usual," he said, taking a seat and scooting it closer to hers.

"Really? That's the best you've got? Use your head!"

The words were like a slap in the man's face, and he flinched, pushing his chair away from hers, back to its original position.

"So you're just going to waltz back out there and

leave more evidence all over the place?" she said, her brows raised, looking at him as if she were questioning one of her children. "If we try your way, and someone comes upon that body sometime, anytime really, we could be blamed for it."

Lloyd admitted to himself he hadn't looked at the problem that way, but he was also still reluctant to believe a body lie on his newly acquired property.

"We're going to have to fess up," she said. Her shoulders slumped and her gaze went empty, staring into the dark abyss of her coffee.

"Huh-uh, no way. We found that money on our land. That makes it ours. I know the inheritance from my daddy allowed us to buy that place, but that case full of cash can go a long way toward making it perfect for us. I'm not handing it over."

"Lloyd, think about it. What if it's stolen? What if it's marked? I'm not going to jail over a few thousand dollars. I got kids to raise."

"We don't know nothing about that money. We surely don't know that it's stolen or marked. You're jumping to conclusions. We can lie low for a while. Maybe rig it so the tow truck driver comes upon those bones. Keep our hands clean."

Becky looked at him with wide eyes. "You may just have a good idea after all. We set it up so it's not us who finds the body, then we have a better chance of being blameless..." Becky trailed off.

Again, Lloyd could see the wheels turning in her

head and felt a rush of pride that he'd finally come up with a hint of a plan she approved of. At the same time, he felt a twinge of guilt at putting that on some hard-working tow driver just doing his job. It wasn't the fairest thing to put somebody through, but it was better than his family being torn apart by some legal mess, or worse, criminal charges. He'd had his run-ins with the law before he met Becky. Mostly due to his lead foot and belief that insurance was for saps. But what he consid-ered to be nuisances might shade the law against him in the face of a dead person on his land.

"Fill up my coffee cup," she said. "And by the time I get the kids up and fed, I'll have it all figured out."

———

Later that morning, Lloyd pulled up to the house a bit later than usual. No one took notice. He passed through the house throwing a wave or a nod to those who saw him. Most were busy with their work. A morning radio show from someone's beat-up boom box echoed through the barren halls. Lloyd recognized the voices of his favorite talk show. He wished he could sit down and laugh along to the banter of the familiar hosts as they played one of his favorite games, "Schnipp Schnapp Schnerpp." But he had work to do, work that needed his complete focus. If he messed this up, he'd never hear the end of it.

Exiting the back door, he came upon a couple of

other workers and nodded as he headed straight to the bulldozer.

"Can't wait to hear the story of how you managed that," one of the workers shouted to him.

"Oh, yeah, it's a doozie," Lloyd hollered back, hoping his tone came off as casually as he intended.

At the spot where he and his future bride fumbled around in frozen fear just hours ago, he quickly spotted the boot. He took his gloves out of his pocket and slid them on his hands before picking up the shoe, hopefully buffing away any trace of his or Becky's touch. He heard a twig snap and froze. The boot in his hand seemed to be vibrating lightly; a low-pitched hum touched his ears, sending a hot shiver down his spine. He heard rustling leaves behind him and broke free of his fixed stance. As he turned towards the sound, something ran past him, brushing his leg. A scream lodged in his throat as a lone turkey scurried by before taking to flight, wings flapping loudly, stirring the air. The disgruntled bird came to rest at the top of the ravine and scratched at the earth for a while before disappearing from view. In the commotion, he had dropped the boot; but fortunately, it remained upright, its remaining contents not spilled. He left it where it lay for the time being.

Lloyd let out a sigh of relief and laughed at himself. Shaking his head, he went back to setting the scene. He burrowed a manageable path with his hands through the thick brush, taking caution to keep things looking as untouched as possible. His fingers landed on the other boot when he reached inside the dark hole and felt around. He pushed his arm further into the dark tunnel, grasping what felt like a pant leg that sat above the shoe and gave it a strong tug. As he did so, an icy blast of air burst from the cave and, from out of the inky den, a face flew toward him. Panic and terror rendered him power-less to move; he remained there, motionless, his eyes unwilling to close no matter how badly he wished to block the terrifying image from his sight. It was the woman who rode in his truck bed the day he made the discovery. She stopped nose-to-nose with him as her mouth opened wide in a silent scream. Deep in her throat, Lloyd could see bugs writhing in a bed of dead leaves. Angry black eyes bulged out from transparent gray skin where dreadful black veins protruded. The vibration returned, this time strong enough to shake the limbs of the trees and rustle the leaves and pebbles on the ground. A dark shadow fell upon the ravine as if some-thing heavy drew across the morning sun. Lloyd's entire body trembled with fear as the woman's breath blasted him again, lifting his tightly fit John Deere cap off his head and into the air where it spun madly before coming to rest on the forest floor. He finally managed to close his eyes.

"NO!" he screamed at the woman, shocked by the sound of his own voice.

The forest grew calm. He didn't dare open his eyes again until he felt a warm beam of light slide across his face. As his sight focused and adjusted to the bright sun, he realized the frightful vision was gone.

He fell back as terror unchained him and relief washed over him. He lay on the bed of leaves until his breathing slowed. The pants he had released from the narrow opening were still clenched tightly in his hand. More bones lay scattered near him, having been freed from their tomb and shroud of faded cloth. Lloyd saw that the clothing was coveralls, but that was all he cared to notice as he gave the scene a quick once over, deciding it would have to do. He wanted nothing more than to be out of this ravine with its bones and angry spirit. He was certain anyone who came into the partially dried creek bed would see the objects and investigate. Becky had told him to make it look like an animal might have dragged the stuff out of the cavern so that if Lloyd was in the presence of another person, he could feign shock at the discovery; and in turn, take any suspicion off himself. He had unwittingly managed to make it look exactly how his fiancée instructed him to.

He turned his back on the nightmare and started to climb out of the ditch when his mind's eye revealed a mistake he had overlooked. Hastily he scrambled back down the incline and retrieved the boot he had left standing as if someone had just stepped out of it. Carefully, he set the boot near a leg of the coveralls and gave the setup a quick glance. His shoulders slumped as he jogged to where his baseball cap came to rest. He snatched up the hat and darted as quickly as he could back to the house.

When he felt that he had moved far enough from the grisly scene in the creek bed, he removed his gloves and, with trembling fingers, dialed the number for Cowboy Towing.

"Howdy, this is Lloyd Hilby. I've gotten myself into a bit of a mess out here at my place in Camelot Crossing. Think I'm gonna need your help." His voice sounded shaky, and he willed himself to calm down as he discussed the details with the dispatcher.

With the second part of Becky's plan now in motion, he headed back to the house to await the tow truck, all the while hoping against hope that he could pull off the rest of the scheme without a hitch.

Chapter Nineteen

A few hours after Lloyd set up the scene and called for a tow, Eduardo Mesena rolled up in his truck. He'd been given a bit of information from dispatch and knew he was facing what would likely be a challenging job. Arduous hauls were his favorite, and he saw each complex tow as another feat he could execute. He usually came away with a good story in the end. He'd towed any number of things, from small cars that found themselves swept up in the flooding of one of the town's many creeks to heavy equipment and everything imaginable in-between. Once, he'd even towed a small airplane.

Eduardo hopped out of the truck as the unfortunate bulldozer operator and homeowner rushed out to greet him. Though a crisp chill penetrated the air, the man's face shown with a gleam of sweat; and when he took a bandanna from his back pocket, Eduardo saw the man's hands trembling. Before introducing himself as Lloyd

Hilby, the man let out a nervous laugh. Eduardo's initial thought was that Lloyd seemed on edge, a squirrelly type, as he continued to fidget—shifting his weight from leg to leg, rubbing his jaw, and crossing his arms—all the while his hands trembling like a scared child. This made Eduardo suspicious from the get-go, and he told himself to keep his guard up. He'd also dealt with his fair share of stolen vehicle recoveries and drunks who tried to worm their way out of sticky situations, and who often wrongly believed the tow truck driver would be willing to cover for them. At least Mr. Hilby hadn't tried to haggle over the cost to get his machinery unstuck … yet.

"How you doing, partner?" Lloyd said as he put his hand out to shake. Eduardo wondered where this man had been living for the last nine months, because hand-shakes were a thing of the past, at least for now. Eduardo gave the man a nod and ignored his outreached hand.

"Oh, right, right, supposed to do the fist or elbow bump thing these days. Sorry, old habits."

"Quite all right. Nice to meet you, Mr. Hilby."

"Call me Lloyd. Got myself in a bit of a pickle," Lloyd said. "Come on out back here and take a look. Gotta admit, I'm more than a touch embarrassed about the whole mess. My tree clearing project ended up being too extreme." Lloyd laughed. Eduardo did not, but his mind was eased some. Maybe the man's nervous demeanor was a symptom of feeling foolish for getting himself in a bind.

"Seems a shame to run down all this nature. Bet you couldn't even see another house from the trees."

"Huh? Oh, yeah. Not a fan of raking. Plus I've got plans for the property. Needed a clean slate to work with."

"Well, I've never met a job I couldn't tackle, so we should be able to get you fixed up here in no time."

Eduardo stood at the edge of the ravine, looking down on the scene below. He wondered if nature hadn't stepped in somehow to prevent the destruction of more of the forest. He wasn't sure what the man's "plans" were, but so far all he'd succeeded in doing was turning a once-beautiful setting into a sea of red dirt. But with the terrain stripped of its trees and undergrowth, it'd be easier to get his truck into position.

"I need to get a closer look down there to see what my best options are."

"Sure, sure, of course,"

At the floor of the creek bed, Eduardo walked slowly, pausing to bend down and get looks from multiple angles, assessing the situation and solving the puzzle in his mind as he went. His customer stood at the front of the machine. Eduardo was taken aback by the line drawn. At the rear of the dozer, nothing but some fallen leaves and rocky juts could be seen atop the red earth. But the front of the machine was thickly shaded with countless trees and brush. Not for the first time since arriving on this site, Eduardo was left wondering why someone would obliterate the forest. Now he contemplated how much wildlife was displaced by this destructive act.

He shook his head slowly as he approached Lloyd. The man was now more fidgety, shifting his weight from leg to leg, arms crossed in front of his body. Eduardo noticed the man's eyes, which he would describe as roguish, were now downright shifty. The man's behavior made Eduardo nervous. He wanted to get to work on pulling the machine out, so he could end his dealings with Lloyd Hilby.

As he bent down at the front of the tractor, he noticed something laying on the ground near the grousers.

"You lose your boots down here?" he asked Lloyd.

"Uh, no, why do you ask?"

Eduardo picked the boot up and immediately dropped it when he saw what the boot was attached to. A surprised yelp escaped his throat, and he stumbled back in shock. The steep wall of the ravine stopped his fall.

"Woah, you all right there, Ed?" Lloyd approached the tow truck driver.

"There's, there's…" Eduardo couldn't find the words. He felt flush, his knees weak.

"A snake? We've been warned about the copperheads around here. Didn't get bit, did ya, Ed?"

Eduardo righted himself and reluctantly moved closer to see if his eyes had played tricks on him.

"It's not a snake; it's bones. Is this some kind of sick joke, man? 'Cus if it is, I'm outta here. You can figure out how to get this thing out yourself or call someone else. This isn't funny."

"Not sure I know what you're getting all worked up about, Ed."

"Those are bones. I'm pretty sure they are human bones."

Lloyd moved in closer and bent over with his hands on his knees.

"Well, I'll be! I think you might be right."

"I'm not towing anything out of here until the police have been called. Why is there a body on your property?"

"Beats me, Ed. We just bought the place a few months ago. If that's a human body, it's been here a lot longer than we have."

"I'm going back to my truck and calling dispatch." Eduardo walked away without waiting for Lloyd.

"Sure thing. Guess I'll call the sheriff's department," Lloyd shouted after Eduardo.

Eduardo waited in his truck until the authorities arrived. He sat trying to calm his nerves, reminding himself to put more trust in his gut feeling from now on.

Chapter Twenty

Craig Mitchell couldn't believe he was being called out on a report of another body found in Camelot Crossing. It wasn't that long ago when investigators finally cleared out of the Weizak property after a long missing girl was found underneath the home's swimming pool. Now he was back out there at another house that was practically a neighbor to the Weizak family. He was certain this would be a false alarm, nothing more than deer bones, a big mistake. He wasn't aware of any missing person cases that were active in the small town and hoped to have things sorted out with a logical explanation in a timely manner.

Driving through the neighborhood, he passed the odd Tudor home where Laura Comb's remains had been unearthed. He found himself wondering how the family was doing and shook his head, as if doing so would have any impact on what he was about to find at another house in the eccentric neighborhood.

He was greeted in the driveway by the familiar face of Eduardo Mesena. The two had become acquaintances as they crossed each other's paths often in their lines of work. Eduardo was visibly shaken, which was unusual for the man. He never seemed too shook up, no matter how bad the accident or situation.

"Eduardo, how's it going? Long time, no see. You the one who called this in?"

"No, the homeowner notified authorities. I stuck around because I'm a witness. Seemed like the right thing to do."

"Yes, sir, appreciate that, but come on, you don't actually believe that what you found is human, do you? I'd say this neighborhood has seen enough of that kind of thing to last them a lifetime."

"I hear you, Deputy, but I'm starting to think Camelot Crossing might be cursed. I'm pretty sure there is a body down in that culvert."

"There's bound to be an explanation that's easier to swallow than unearthed remains. Let's go have a look."

"Sure thing. Here comes the owner now. Something seems a little off about this guy."

Craig Mitchell didn't have time to respond or ponder the last thing that Eduardo said. The homeowner was upon him, his hand extended for a handshake. He caught himself as he came upon the two men and withdrew his hand.

"My apologies, Deputy…?" Lloyd said, fishing for the officer's name.

"Craig Mitchell. And you are?"

"Lloyd Hilby. Nice to meet you, Deputy Mitchell."

"Likewise. Eduardo tells me you two may have stumbled upon some questionable findings. Mind showing me where?"

"Yeah, right this way. I'm not as convinced as Ed here that the bones belong to a person; but then again, I'm no expert on the matter."

When the three reached the edge of the culvert, Lloyd pointed down to the area where the boots lay.

"Right down there, in front of the bulldozer, Deputy."

"All right, you two stay here, please. I'll check things out." Craig sidestepped down the embankment and pulled some gloves from his pocket. He spotted the boot and took his phone out, snapping a few pictures to document the scene before he took a closer look.

"Well, would you look at that?" Craig said to no one but himself and the remains that lay before him. Wrong in his assumption, he was floored to see that another body had indeed been discovered in Camelot Crossing.

He spoke into the radio clipped to his shoulder, asking for backup, and made his way out of the ravine. When he reached the top, he said, "Well, gentlemen, I'm going to have to ask you to stay away from the site. I believe we may be dealing with human remains. We need to keep the scene from being contaminated while we sort things out."

"So, it really is, er, was, a person?" Lloyd asked.

"Can't be a hundred percent certain, but I'm convinced enough to have called in some help."

Chapter Twenty-One

Birdie gave little thought to the activity behind the Clarkson home after Iva brought it to her attention. She had far too much to worry about inside the home to concern herself with the happenings on another property. She stood in the kitchen stirring a pot of bone broth. As the sun set, the darkened sky flashed with red and blue strobes. The colored beams bounced off the walls of the kitchen, drawing her away from the task. The curious commotion had intensified since she last glanced out the window. Flashing lights from emergency vehicles lit up the forest. Through the barren trees, she saw a flurry of activity now on both sides of the ravine. As she stood watching, the kitchen door leading outside slammed open, startling her.

She walked to the door to close it and saw Wren at the edge of the patio. Wren turned and motioned for Birdie to follow her. The lights pulsed through Wren's form, giving her fiery movement. Birdie quickly shut the door, ignoring her sister's attempt to lure her outside. She stood with her back against the closed door and tried to calm her nerves, breathing deeply.

"What's going on back there, Aunt Birdie?" Marlow asked as he stood peering out the kitchen window.

Birdie did not hear the boy approach. The sound of his voice gave her more of a scare than the door opening, and she screamed. Marlow paid no mind to her cry, nor to her trembling body.

"They found another body," Iva announced, entering the room and joining her brother.

"What makes you think that, Iva?"

"It's Mom. Mom's body is back there." The teen uttered the word's matter-of-factly, her tone detached.

Birdie snapped the burner off and went to the window. She grabbed Iva by the shoulders, turning the teen to face her.

"Iva, why would you say such a thing?" Birdie shook the girl gently, almost believing she could shake the irrational thoughts out of Iva's mind.

"She told me." Iva's eyes were void of emotion.

"That's enough! First your grandmother, now you?" Birdie yelled.

"It's true. She told me. In a dream last night, she said she was finally coming home." A tear slid down Iva's cheek; the emotion behind it still did not show on her face.

"What are you talking about? Are you running a fever again?" Birdie felt the girl's forehead.

"No, Aunt Birdie, she has talked to me a lot. More when I was younger. In my dreams, she would sing me a song, or play a game with me. She hasn't been in my dreams for a long time, but last night she came back."

Birdie had too many questions springing up in her head; she couldn't decide what to say next. She wasn't given the chance, however, when the doorbell chimed.

"Don't go anywhere, you hear me? It's probably just a package delivery, but I am not done with you."

Birdie was so lost in thought, she didn't check the peephole to see who stood on the other side of the door. She opened it to a man in uniform and a man in a suit. The men's faces were partly hidden by masks, but she was certain she did not know them.

The man in the sheriff's uniform spoke first. "Good evening, ma'am. You wouldn't happen to be Lula Clarkson, would you?"

"No, um, that's my mother. I am Birdie Clarkson, her daughter," she replied.

"I'm Sheriff Doug Rayne, and this is Dr. Samuel Kaiser. Do you mind if we come in? We've got some things of importance to discuss with your mother."

"Yes, of course, Well, I mean you can come in, but my mother is very sick. She really shouldn't see visitors right now. I'm not sure if she is still contagious, but she is very weak, and well…" Birdie trailed off but opened the door wider, allowing the men entry.

The sheriff removed his hat as he entered the house. The entryway to the Clarkson home was large, but shrunk in the presence of the group, and the air felt heavy, tense. The pressure and claustrophobic atmosphere deepened considerably as Iva and Marlow entered.

"Is there someplace we can all sit?" Dr. Kaiser spoke up.

"Oh, yes, sure, this way. Follow me," Birdie said, flustered.

The group moved to the cozy family room off the kitchen. Birdie was still unable to process what was happening and thus lost all sense of hospitality. She sat on the couch beside Iva and Marlow and forgot to offer a seat to their visitors. After an awkward pause, the sheriff and the doctor sat themselves.

"Ms. Clarkson, I'm a medical examiner for Payne County," Dr. Kaiser said.

Birdie sat in dumbfounded silence.

"Do you know a Wren Clarkson?" the sheriff asked.

Birdie still couldn't find words.

"Wren is our mom," Marlow said. Birdie looked at the boy wide-eyed.

"You folks may have been aware of some activity over the past several hours on the property that sits behind this home…"

Birdie managed to choke out a response. "Yes, uh, yes we have."

"Well, ma'am, children," the Sheriff continued. "I

regret to inform you, but the remains of a person were found in the culvert. Identification found at the scene suggests the body could be that of Wren Clarkson. A driver's license was found on the remains. Of course, that's not irrefutable evidence."

"We need to confirm the identity. Are any of you currently in contact with Wren Clarkson?" the medical examiner asked.

"No, no, we aren't. My sister, the children's mother, left several years ago. None of us have heard from her since."

"I see. When exactly did your sister leave?" asked Sheriff Rayne, removing a notepad and pen from a pocket.

"It was in early 2011," Birdie started.

"January 31st of 2011," Marlow interjected.

"I see. And what were the circumstances related to her departure?"

Birdie didn't like the direction this conversation was going in and wanted to distance her niece and nephew. "Iva, Marlow, maybe you two could go check on Gram?"

Marlow started to rise, but Iva grabbed his wrist.

"I'm sure Gram is sleeping, and I think my brother and I should hear this." Iva's tone was direct and determined.

Marlow said nothing but sat back down next to his sister. He slid his wrist up from his sister's grasp and took her hand.

"So you never filed a missing person report on Ms.

Clarkson in all this time?" the sheriff asked.

"No, my sister was, um, a free spirit I guess you could say," Birdie said timidly, struggling to find her voice. "She lived by her own rules. She took several items with her, including her suitcase. We've always lived under the assumption that she left on her own."

"But she's never been in contact after that time?" the sheriff questioned further, his inflection lowering with each word.

Birdie registered an emphasis the sheriff placed on the word never and realized how cold this must sound to an outsider, especially one who wasn't aware of Wren's whims, and her body stiffened. She adjusted the sleeve of her sweater nervously and plucked a nonexistent piece of fluff from her pants, giving herself a moment to consider how to respond to the question

"No, she hasn't," Birdie whispered. The reply sounded pathetic and inadequate to her.

"There are a few ways we can go about confirming the identity of the remains," Dr. Kaiser said. "If you have dental records for Ms. Clarkson, they would be a first helpful step."

"We've all gone to Dr. Tipton our whole lives. I assume he would have them," Birdie answered.

"That's good. Do you mind signing a release for us, so we can access those records quickly?"

"Of course, anything we can do to help."

The sheriff and doctor remained for another half hour discussing the process. Birdie sensed that the reality of the implications the news brought fell on Iva and Marlow like a heavy weight as they sat silently listening to the conversation with numb expressions. As soon as Sheriff Rayne and Dr. Kaiser departed, the teens disappeared to their bedrooms without a word.

Birdie paced through the house. Disjointed thoughts spun relentlessly in her mind as she processed the news and pondered how to tell her mother. Lula was so frail and sickly that Birdie was afraid of what telling her might mean to her health. But she knew she couldn't keep it from her mother. Dr. Kaiser indicated it could be a matter of days before they would know for sure if the body was Wren's. Part of her was afraid her mother might not make it for a few more days.

She thought of Iva's admission that came at the very moment the two officials stood outside the front door. Could Wren have died so long ago? And so close to her family home? It didn't seem possible. Guilt wracked Birdie forcefully. She felt dizzy and flush. The room spun, forcing her to grab onto the farmhouse sink as she choked back acidic bile that rose in her throat. Maybe they should have done more to search for Wren; to search for answers. They had all failed Wren, especially Birdie. No matter how hard Birdie tried to shield her parents from Wren's misdeeds, her efforts had been for nothing.

As her balance returned, she moved to stand at the kitchen window; looking at the flashing lights, she saw Wren emerge from the woods again. Her sister still held the pink bundle, but she was not focused on it. Her eyes locked on Birdie and would not let go. Birdie held her sister's gaze for as long as she could stand. In an attempt to quiet her mind, she returned to the stock cooling on the stove top and turned the burner back on, waiting until the liquid bubbled. She turned off the burner and scooped the hot broth into a bowl; then placed it on a tray along with a spoon, some juice, and water and climbed the stairs to check on her mother and have a most difficult conversation.

Upstairs, in Lula's bedroom, the air felt different, smelled different—lighter, cleaner, and fresher. It was unnerving but Birdie couldn't put her finger on what it was making her feel that way. She was shocked to see her mother sitting up in bed. The television was on, and Lula held the remote as she flipped through the channels.

"More soup?" Lula questioned her daughter.

Birdie was taken aback by the drastic change in her mother. Lula's face was still pale, but brighter and fuller. Her voice sounded clearer, and she sat upright in bed, a huge improvement over her condition for the past couple of weeks.

"Yes, Mom, more soup," Birdie spoke as she crossed the room with the tray and placed it on the side table. "You are looking better this evening."

"I'm feeling a bit better as well. Did I hear the door-bell ring?

Birdie feared the news would send Lula's health into a downward spiral just as she seemed to be turning a corner. She contemplated her options. Scenarios shuffled through her mind quickly. How she wished she had someone to help her through this. Finally, she spoke.

"Yes, it was the doorbell, Mom, I need to tell you something that isn't going to be easy to hear." Birdie spoke slowly as she searched for words.

Lula grew impatient. "Spit it out. Is it the children? I thought they were feeling better."

"No, it isn't about the children. Iva and Marlow are fine."

"Well, that's a relief."

"Mom, they found a body, skeletal remains rather, in the forest." Birdie's voice was barely a whisper.

"Another body?" Lula questioned, pausing to catch her breath. "How can there be another body in these woods? When did Camelot Crossing become a cemetery? Do they know who it is?"

"Mom, this is really hard for me."

"All right, I get it, but go on."

"The people at the door were the sheriff and a coroner."

"Okay, that makes sense, I guess, but what were they doing at our door?"

Lula's speech slowed and the end of her question came out in a whisper as Birdie saw a spark of knowing in her mother's eyes. Before she could answer, her mother spoke again.

"Wait, do they ... do they think it is Wren?" Lula gasped.

"Well, it hasn't been confirmed, but there were items

with the body that point to it being Wren."

"What kind of items?"

"There was a purse with the body, and inside the purse was a driver's license, Wren's driver's license."

"No," Lula said, shaking her head. "That's impossible. Why would Wren's body be out there?" Her mother struggled to get up.

"Lie down, Mom." Birdie went to her mother, gently holding her hand and helping her ease back down against the pillows. "I know this is a shock—"

"It's more than a shock, Birdie. It's ludicrous. How could her body be out there on our property? When was it put there? Did someone dump her out there? Birdie, what is happening?"

"I wish I had answers for you, Mom, but I don't," she said, rubbing her mother's hands in an act that soothed herself likely more than it did her mother. "I signed some papers so they could get Wren's dental records. They are going to do a comparison. Until then, there is nothing more to say about it."

"No, I don't believe it. It isn't possible," Lula lamented. "My girl couldn't have been out there this whole time."

"I don't know, Mom. Think of the weather the night she left."

"Stop that! Stop that talk right now, Birdie," Lula snapped, pulling her hands away from her daughter's grasp and pushing herself up.

"I'm sorry, Mom. The sheriff said they hoped to

know more in a few days."

"A few days? They come into my home saying my baby girl has been lying dead on my very own property, but it will take days to make sure? That's not fair of them, Birdie." A note of resignation sounded in Lula's voice signaling to Birdie that her mother was digesting the news and its implications. Tears built in Lula's eyes as she sat slowly shaking her head from side to side, her gaze unfocused.

"I know. I'm so sorry. I shouldn't have said anything until I had more information. You can't get worked up like this. You're sweating buckets. Lie back down. I'll get you some Nyquil; you need to sleep if you want this rebound to last."

"How am I supposed to sleep with this news wearing on me?"

Lula was crying, and Birdie felt horrible for sharing the dreadful information while her mother was in such a weakened state. She went to the bathroom and found the bottle of cold medicine. Instead of filling the little plastic cup up to the line, she topped the cap off with the thick, green liquid. Her mom might need a bit more to help her sleep tonight.

She carefully walked back to Lula's bed, trying not to spill the medicine. Lula didn't notice the cap was filled to the rim. She dutifully took the medicine and handed the cup back to her daughter.

"Can you stay with me for a bit, Bird? Just until I fall asleep. I don't want to be alone right now."

"Of course, Mom. I'll be right here. I'm so sorry."

"I don't understand. If it is her, why did she leave?" Lula asked as her eyelids drooped heavily.

Birdie did not want to answer that question, so she said nothing.

Within minutes, Birdie could tell that her mother had fallen asleep as her breath evened out, the tension left her body, and her head sunk into the pillow. She quietly rose from the chair next to the bed and pulled the blankets up, gently tucking them around the tiny woman's shoulders. Next, she bent over and kissed her mother's forehead before turning to leave. As she slowly closed the bedroom door, she heard a text message come in on her phone and withdrew it from her sweater pocket.

UNKNOWN: *It's now or never, Birdie-Bird.*"

She crammed her phone back into her pocket and went to the hall bathroom to ready herself for what she predicted might be a restless night's sleep.

———

Lula slept well that night. Birdie did not. She lay awake, listening to the sound on the floor below her. Marlow could be heard excitedly yelling to his friends, the group, no doubt, deeply involved in a game. It was hard to know if the boy was intentionally distracting his mind from the news delivered that afternoon, or if he had become numb to the troubles his mother exposed him to, now apparently from the grave. When his words quieted, she could hear Iva's soft murmurs, likely Facetiming a friend. It saddened her to realize she had no idea to whom Iva turned for comfort. How she wished she could go to them, console them and be the shoulder they cried on.

A steady stream of tears slid down her face and dampened her pillow. She was unable to discern if she cried for herself, for Iva and Marlow, or for her mother. One thing she did know was that her tears were not for her sister. She no longer had to live in fear that Wren would return and lay waste to the life she had built for her family. While that knowledge should have comforted her, it only made things worse—for she had no clue how she could ever mend the disconnect between herself and the children. None of this had ever been part of her plan. She was not the mother figure she believed herself to be, and she now feared Wren might have shaped her children's lives better than she had.

At some point, after even the voices of Iva and Marlow had gone silent, weariness overtook Birdie, and she began to drift off. Before her conscious mind closed its door, she felt a shift on the bed and heard the light snoring of her sister. Instead of keeping her back to Wren as she usually did, she turned to face her and fell asleep feeling light, warm breaths dry her tears.

Shadows reached far across the room when she woke. She wasn't granted a moment to see how late she had slept in. The shrill ringtone of her phone had stirred her —the sheriff delivering confirmation, along with a grievous finding.

Chapter Twenty-Two

Victor Hall parked his Mercedes in his reserved spot at the back of the clinic. Aside from his new car, the small parking lot was vacant. It was early still; the sun had just begun to brighten the sky on what was to be an unseasonably warm winter day. Victor was always the first to the office even when the patient load was light or nonexistent, the virus preventing many from treatment for back pain, stiff necks, or whatever ailed them. His dedication stemmed partly from a desire to get out of the house, away from his wife and the pressures she felt with the added responsibility of assisting in the education of their children.

But the most pressing reason was to give him time to check the books, the bank statements and mail, anything that might tip someone off that he was still regularly helping himself to an ill-gotten share of the practice's profits. Of course, the calendar didn't fill up as it had prior to March 2020. If the disruptive virus wasn't controlled soon, he wasn't certain the practice would stay afloat. Once the clinic really started to struggle, he was concerned he'd be found out. With the pandemic tightening purse strings, absent funds might be missed more than they had when it was thriving. Dr. Parson was getting up there in years, looking at retirement and weighing his options on selling the practice; often lamenting that he should have cut and run before the safer at-home edicts were implemented.

"If only I'd had a crystal ball," Dr. Parson would say as he reviewed the sparse calendar each day.

The senior doctor's attention to details he'd often left in other's hands was becoming a concern, but Victor was certain he'd socked away enough money to buy the man out. He never felt an ounce of guilt; he actually relished in the knowledge that Dr. Parson himself unwittingly funded Victor's big career break. He just had to keep the man off his scent until the deal was done. Once the Hall name took top billing in the practice, the embezzled funds would be of no consequence.

He stooped to pick up the stack of newspapers left at the back entrance before swiping his entry card and disarming the security system. So few patients were seen in-office these days, it made no sense to continue getting so many lobby copies. Perhaps it was a sign of optimism on behalf of the office manager that the waiting room would soon be full again. Perhaps it was a lazy oversight. It wasn't until he dropped the newspapers on the break room counter before turning the coffee pot on that he noticed the headline.

Body of Long-Missing Woman Discovered
Could engraved cuff links solve the mystery of her disappearance?

The large bold letters screaming the shocking headline didn't necessarily pique his interest, and he went about filling one of the carafes with water. Another perk to being the first one in was making the coffee exactly as he liked it. He turned the tap on and began filling the pot when the photo beside the byline caught his eye. He stared at the image while the water overflowed the coffee pot. It was Wren Clarkson, his former lover and partner in crime. He dropped the carafe in the sink, shattering it, as his eyes fell upon the words:

The remains of Wren Clarkson, a Stillwater resident who went missing in 2011, have been found mere yards from her family home.

Any notion Victor had to make coffee or clean up the shattered glass disappeared as he fumbled for the top copy of the newspaper and continued reading. His eyes scanned the front page frantically, focusing on random words that jumped out at him and intensified his panic.

… coroner's report indicated the woman was with child at the time of her death.

A gift-wrapped box containing cuff links engraved with the initials V. H. were …

… no official cause of death …

… seeking information from anyone who might have …

Attempts to contact the Clarkson family for a statement have gone unanswered.

Beads of sweat sprung forth on his brow and above his lips. He tugged on his tie and loosened his collar. This development could prove disastrous. A barrage of terrifying thoughts flooded his mind and he did not hear Dr. Parson enter the clinic until the man's words cast him back, with a start, to the moment at hand.

"Good morning, Victor. I want you to meet Mr. Clay. He's an accountant I've hired to deal with some discrepancies in the books. I'm hoping your morning is free enough that you can sit down with us and get started on an audit."

"Oh, um, yeah, sure. I think I can carve out some time. I wasn't aware there was a problem, I mean, business has certainly slowed with all this *safer at home* nonsense, but—"

"No, while I've taken a cursory glance, there are some inconsistencies that don't add up. Have you heard of a company called RegeneSource? We've been paying them quite large sums for a few years now and I've never heard of them, nor do I have any idea what they do."

Dr. Parson's tone was far from accusatory, but Victor knew he would be discovered. RegeneSource was a dummy corporation whose only employee was Victor himself. There would be no patsy to throw under the bus, no way out of this mess. His house of cards wasn't crumbling, it was imploding. On weak legs, he slowly made his way to his office. He was unaware of anything around him. Images of himself in an orange prison suit clouded his vision and a ringing in his ears blocked out all sound. His clothes were steeped in a cold sweat. It wouldn't take long for the connection between him and Wren Clarkson to come to light, especially once his complex skimming plan was unraveled. Wren had been used as a red herring, a distraction to hide the real embezzlement he was orchestrating. All his schemes to recoup the twenty-five thousand dollars from her had failed. It was a fool's errand; he didn't need the money, but his arrogance and pride had taken a hit.

He was left rattled and without a plan. Victor Hall always had a plan. Of all the outcomes shuffling through his mind, the one notion that shook him the most was knowing his wife and children would be shamed because of his actions. He could not bear the thought of his family suffering the humiliation of the embezzlement, his connection to a body being discovered, and his relation-ship to that body—regardless of how many years had passed. *With child? His child?* There was only one way to spare his family from the impending ostracism.

He took a few minutes to gain his composure, fanned his face with a patient chart that lay on his desk, got control of his breathing, and grabbed a face mask before making his way down the hall to the conference room where Dr. Parson sat with the accountant. Both men were hunched over piles of spreadsheets, concentrating so deeply on their task he had to knock on the opened door to get their attention.

"Sorry to interrupt," he started. "I'm going to keep my distance and leave this mask on because it seems as if I've been exposed to the virus. Can't believe I've made it this far without a scare." He did his best to act casual. "I think it'd be wise for me to head home. I need to help my wife with the kids. They've both got a cough and a fever. To be honest, she's freaking out a bit. Don't want to expose you two anymore than I may have already, so I'm going to head home and lie low until I can get tested."

"Oh, well, that is truly unfortunate," Dr. Parson said, rising from his seat. He caught himself before he moved closer to Victor. "Yes, you're one-hundred-percent correct, go home, help with the kids and take care of yourself. I'll have Amanda send the exposure text to those on the schedule for the next few days. She'll have to spray a few cans of Lysol around, but better safe than sorry. Go on, Victor. We can take things from here."

Victor reveled in a moment of relief. At least that part had gone well. Just a few more potentially sticky situations to navigate before he considered himself home free. He didn't bother gathering anything to take with him that he could work on at home. His fingers grazed the photo that sat on his desk as he took a deep breath and a tear slid down his face. The photo had been taken a couple of years ago, the smiling faces of his children, wife, and himself; the perfect image the world was presented with. Grief and regret punched him in the chest, forcing bitter bile to fill his mouth. He made it to the wastebasket and removed his mask just in time.

Normally, he would clean the can himself, but there was no time nor need for that. He wiped his mouth with the back of his hand, grabbed his keys, and left the clinic, knowing he would never return.

At home, relief touched him again when he found the house empty. Even the family's new pup was gone. They had recently adopted the mutt. It seemed like the right time. Everyone could devote as much time as needed to its care and upbringing since the world had closed down. The dog's absence meant his wife and kids had gone to the park or for a walk. Not knowing when they'd return urged him to rush through the next steps of his plan.

In his closet, he ran his hand blindly over the top shelf, his fingers quickly landing on a set of lockbox keys. His hand guided the keys directly below him to the fire safe on the floor. Inside the safe were important documents: social security cards, passports, and such. The paperwork covered the handgun at the bottom of the safe. He took the gun and a handful of ammunition and shoved them in his pocket. He left the box open, knowing his wife would soon need many of the records it held. The only real reason he ever kept it locked was the gun. They did the right things as parents, keeping the weapon locked and secured from their children. His mind went to all the things he had done right—all the times he'd been unselfish, truthful, loyal—and realized all those moments would now be overshadowed by the few things he'd done that were horribly wrong. What a waste he was.

He shook the musings out of his head and set his mind on autopilot. He could not think about the steps that needed to be taken; he would just take action without thought. Otherwise, he might balk. This was his chance to get one last thing right. Keeping his eyes down so as to not take in the sights that made up his daily life, he made his way to the garage.

Once there, he took the helmet off the seat of his motorcycle. His wife had begged him to get rid of the bike when their oldest was born. He'd stubbornly held on to the symbol of his freedom, even though he rarely, if ever, drove the thing. She insisted he wear a helmet whenever he did take it out for a drive. Today, he laid the helmet on a shelf close by. There was no need for a helmet today. He straddled the bike and backed it out of the garage. The cycle roared to life and Victor drove away from his home, never to return.

Out on the highway, he drove mindlessly, soaking in the feeling of the wind pressing against him and the sun on his face. His fuel gauge told him the tank would run dry soon, so he took the first right turn off the country highway and drove until the gravel roads became too challenging to navigate. A faded No Trespassing sign, riddled with rusty bullet holes, dangled on a barbed wire fence. Weeds sprung up between the worn tire marks, telling him this road was rarely traversed and would therefore be a good place to die. He sidled the motor-cycle behind a tall, thick tangle of brushwood and scrub. The gnarled growth was encrusted in the red dirt from which it grew, giving it an eerie, orange hue. There, he lowered the bike, sure it would be difficult to spot by the few travelers that meandered down the dusty, overgrown roadway. The spot was rural enough that no one would find him for some time. He certainly wouldn't be found out if for some reason he botched the job. The last thing he needed was some good Samaritan rancher to find him injured and maimed but alive enough for doctors to spare his life. He ducked under the barbed fence. On the other side of the spiky barrier, he straightened his tie and jacket, then walked several yards to a bank of trees. He settled into the cool shade of a large oak tree, pulled out his phone, and sent a message to his wife:

V: ***I love you and the kids with all my heart. Please forgive me.***

He did not wait for her to reply; he turned the phone off and, for good measure, smashed it against the tree. As the crack of the gun shattered the quiet sounds of nature, dozens of crows erupted from the tree, blacking out the sky. Victor did not hear their angry cries. After some time, those same crows returned to feast on the body of Victor Hall.

Chapter Twenty-Three

UNKNOWN: ***Get up! Don't let her die alone. She needs you. She needs to know.***

The text notification woke Birdie from a restless sleep. Rather than feeling the usual indignation at the intrusive text, she felt panic. There was no second guessing who "she" was. Birdie got out of bed quickly and ran for the bedroom door. From the attic landing, the house was silent and dark. She made her way down the stairs to her mother's room, where she heard voices on the other side of the door. Fear coursed through her body, quickening her pulse. She froze, ear to the door, breath held in her lungs, trying to make out what was being said; and more importantly, who was speaking. The voice sounded too subdued, but she was certain it belonged to a woman.

Birdie reached for the doorknob, but the door was thrown open, the knob yanked from her grip. Wren stood next to their mother's bed. Neither woman seemed to notice Birdie. She stood, unable to move, fixated on her sister.

"Wren, I've missed you so. Where have you been all this time?" Lula's voice was hoarse; her words came out slowly, every few words left hanging, halted by quick gulps of air. It was painful to hear Lula struggling to speak to someone who couldn't actually be there.

"What's that you've got there?"

Wren did not answer, which made Lula's words all the more disturbing.

"A baby?"

Again, Lula responded to an unheard answer. While the scene unfolding before her was unsettling, this question sent a fiery chill up Birdie's spine. She had chosen her words carefully when she broke the news to her mother. The revelation had the effect Birdie had feared. Lula's rebound from her illness evaporated, and her condition deteriorated at a brutal speed. Birdie did not regret withholding the shocking news that Wren had been with child when she died. Her knees buckled with Lula's next words. The coroner had not shared the gender of the unborn child.

"A girl! Oh, Wren!" Lula tried to sit up, her arms reaching out to welcome Wren's bundle—a gesture she'd made countless times when Iva and Marlow were infants. For a moment, it was as if Lula was released from the pain and limitations of her sickly decline.

Wren made no move to hand over what she held. Lula fell back into the bed, empty-handed.

"Why can't you just tell me? I've missed you so." Her chest rose and fell rapidly. "I'm so tired. So ready, but I can't leave until I know why. Why did you go?"

Tears burned Birdie's cheeks as she stood and watched what she knew were her mother's final moments of life. She clenched her eyes shut, wanting to block out the devastation she was witnessing.

"Don't go, Wren," Lula croaked.

Birdie opened her eyes and was met by the face of her sister, so close that she blocked the entire view of the room beyond. Wren let out a silent wail that hit Birdie's face with a force and pushed her back against the wall. Birdie remained frozen in fear until she heard her mother's voice again. Lula seemed to sense Birdie's presence now and called for her.

"Birdie, come help me, please. Tell me why she left."

Birdie recoiled and slowly sidestepped Wren, crossing the room to her mother's bed. The walls pressed in on her, shrinking the space with a suffocating grip. She sat on the edge of Lula's bed, taking her hands; then fought to keep herself from withdrawing as Lula's frigid skin sent a jolting chill up her arm.

"Birdie, tell me, please," her mother implored in a whispered, fading voice.

"Mom, I told you already, the body they found in the woods is Wren—"

"No!" Lula's tone was fervent and raw. "Why did she leave? I need to know."

"I'm sorry, Mom. I don't know!"

"You do know. Your father told me you knew. Wren says it isn't her secret to share. Please, Birdie."

The simple act of forming words left Lula depleted. She collapsed back again, eyes closed, as she struggled for air. The woman's desperate attempt to cling to life was heartbreaking, but Birdie could still not bring herself to speak the words her mother needed to hear.

Shame and guilt seized Birdie, and she collapsed onto the bed, just wanting to lay with her mother, to feel the comfort and safety she felt as a child when she turned to her for solace. How had she strayed so far from what she envisioned for herself, her parents, the kids? How had she let one foolish decision beget such dire consequence?

Her mother needed her now. As hard as it would be to tell the truth, she owed it to her mother, as she had owed it to her father as he lay dying. Birdie gathered herself and resolved to do the right thing, no matter how painful it would be. She took her mother's cold hand and bent over her mother's tiny figure to kiss her forehead. A shadow slipped over Birdie as she leaned in to whisper in her mother's ear. Before she could speak, Lula's eyes fluttered, and she spoke.

"Both my girls here with me." Lula's words were barely a whisper.

"She left for a man, a man and some money. She wanted to start a new life, away from here, away from us." Birdie struggled to expose the cold truth, the reality that none of them were important enough to Wren. That she would abandon her children, her family, with such indifference. That a fleeting romance and a paltry amount of ill-gotten cash was enough for her to walk away from her own children and a family that loved her. Birdie kept it hidden so long she expected some sense of unburdening, some relief, might come with the revelation.

Birdie looked up and saw that Wren had taken Lulu's other hand. Wren's cold eyes bore into Birdie. Just as she had felt when her father lay dying, Birdie knew the only way to quiet Wren's fury was to give up her most tightly held secret, one she believed she would take to her own grave. Tears poured from her eyes, falling into her mother's long, silver hair as she leaned in and whispered the same words she had revealed to her father five years ago. She laid bare the vile and unforgivable truth.

Lula gasped; her eyes tightly closed. Birdie waited for the torrent of emotion to spill out of her mother, but Lula had nothing left to say. Her lungs emptied slowly, a whisper of breath, and then nothing more.

Birdie lay with her dead mother for some time. The weight of the air lightened, and she no longer sensed that she was not alone. She didn't have the energy to do what needed to be done. Ever since her father died, her mother repeatedly pressed upon Birdie the steps to take when her time came. Birdie knew exactly where her mother's DNR was and knew which authorities she should call. What her mother hadn't shown her was how to cope with the pain and how to share that pain with Iva and Marlow. The burden was so heavy. She was now the only person the children had left. She couldn't imagine herself living up to that commitment, even though she had been striving to do so since Iva was born. For the first time in her life, she wished Wren was there.

The sun would be up within two hours, so Birdie opted to wait to tell the children, to call 911, to do anything other than lay with her mother.

———

Birdie woke to a light knocking on the bedroom door. The sun broke through the window, lighting Lula's peaceful face and sweeping across her long, white hair. Iva did not wait for Birdie to open the door; she let herself in as Birdie rose to console her before she saw her grandmother in her final state of repose. Birdie wasn't prepared for what the girl had to say.

"She's gone, isn't she? I had a dream. Mom told me that Gram was gone." The timbre of her voice rose to a place that reminded Birdie of Iva as a young girl, the trill voice, breaking with sobs.

Birdie rushed to hug the girl, but Iva pushed her away.

"What did you do to her?" The small child was gone. Iva's words hit Birdie like a slap.

"What do you mean? I didn't *do* anything to her. She was sick, Iva. It was her time."

Iva didn't respond; she turned and ran from the room. Birdie heard her pounding on Marlow's door, then she heard hushed murmurs from the two.

Birdie knew they would not seek comfort from her, so she retrieved the folder containing Lula's final wishes from the nightstand drawer and took it downstairs to make phone calls.

Later that morning when two people from the funeral home arrived to take Lula's body, Birdie asked that the body bag not be zipped up to cover her mother's face. This detail had been overlooked by Lula when she wrote her directives, but Birdie couldn't stand the thought of her mother being plummeted into darkness, depriving her one last chance to witness the grandchildren she adored, her beloved home and garden. A gentle breeze enlivened Lula's wind chimes as the attendants lifted her over the home's threshold; sounding a mournful dirge that echoed through the air.

The three remaining Clarksons stood on the front porch, unable to believe that their devoted matriarch was gone. Marlow held his sister as she wept, the boy's face unflinching, stoic. For the first time, Birdie saw the man he would become and wondered how she hadn't noticed he now stood half a foot taller than his older sister. She wanted to embrace them both, longed to be a part of their grieving. Neither teen reached out for her. She stood alone and watched the two turn to the door,

Marlow dutifully opening it for Iva as the hearse made its way down the winding drive.

Birdie's knees buckled, and she collapsed on the steps of the porch as waves of sadness struck her. She didn't know which was more painful and devastating—the loss of her mother, or the loss of Iva and Marlow. Loneliness had been a fixture in Birdie's life, but never had she felt more forsaken and dispirited. She allowed herself some time to purge some of the sorrow. Then she forced the anguish down and went into the house to do what she knew needed to be done next.

Chapter Twenty-Four

"I'll be back in a bit," Birdie shouted to the kids. Iva and Marlow were upstairs in their rooms, privately grappling with the loss of their grandmother. They likely didn't hear Birdie and probably wouldn't miss her or notice she had left.

She climbed in her car, and for the first time since that day so many years ago, she was alone. Her sister was not sitting in the backseat with her bundle of blankets. Of all the times Birdie had wished she could be alone in the car, doing so now fell flat.

She had a singular goal in mind that she believed so important, it took precedence over remaining at her parents' home on the off chance her niece and nephew needed her. There was one thing that had to be done to protect them all from an awful truth that she never wanted to come to light.

Arriving at her quiet, dark home, she parked her car askew in the driveway, not bothering to lock the car doors as she ran to the porch. Her hands shook with anxious energy, making it difficult for her to unlock the front door. Finally, the key slid into the lock, and she flung the door open, dropping her purse and keys onto the ground just inside the threshold. She rushed to her bedroom, leaving the front door ajar. The television did not turn on as she had come to anticipate, and there were no shoes in the doorway to her room. She flipped on the light and took notice of the neatly made bed.

In her closet, she pulled boxes down from the top shelf, tearing them open and dumping their contents on the floor. She mumbled to herself, her condemning words escaping under her breath. Though if anyone had been listening, they would find it impossible to decipher what she said. How had she been so careless with such an important item? Why had she held on to it all this time when it was the one thing that could seal her fate as it had sealed her sister's so long ago? She cursed herself for not getting rid of it, and for storing it so haphazardly that she couldn't remember where she kept it hidden.

At the time, she couldn't wait to brandish the evidence; show everyone how little it took for Wren to abandon her children. As the years went by, she still thought she'd have the chance to do so; had even fantasized about the moment when Wren returned, and Birdie could expose her for being a selfish and unfit mother. It was the only concrete evidence Birdie had to prove to them all how right she was. Never had she given thought to the possibility that Wren's life had ended. When her sister didn't return, Birdie's feelings of righteousness multiplied.

Of course, Birdie believed her sister was having an affair and had strong suspicions that Wren and the married chiropractor were the embezzlers Euphemia felt so certainly were bilking funds from the clinic. She clung to the belief that Wren saw her chance in that text message and had abandoned her children, her life, willingly. Birdie's convictions only wavered when their father died. She fully expected Wren to make a shocking entrance, one that would overshadow even the burial of the Clarkson patriarch. When she didn't show up for their father's funeral, Birdie began to wonder if Wren had met with misfortune. If Birdie were honest with herself, by that time she cared very little about Wren's fate.

Her subconscious never allowed her to believe she had done the right thing, however. The conjurings of Wren poisoned her act of courage. The same madness that pushed her to execute such an ill-conceived and consequential deed forced her to exist with her self-induced retribution. When she couldn't ascribe blame upon her flawed psyche, paranoia seeped in. When you can't trust yourself, you can trust no one.

She rummaged through the piles of emptied boxes, tossing aside old purses, scarves, ticket stubs, photos, and the like. Relics of a once-promising life lie scattered around her.

"Where is it?" she spoke out loud. "Where did I put it?" A groan of frustration built in her throat as tears spilled down her face. She crawled across the floor, sweeping memorabilia and papers out of the way when she knelt on something hard that sent a bolt of pain through her leg. As she fell back clutching her knee, she spotted the item she was so desperately searching for. She stared at it for a moment, afraid to reach out and touch it. It was much bigger than she remembered it being and so vastly different from the one she carried today. She stared in wonderment at the ubiquitous object that had altered the lives of so many. Who was she back then? How had she convinced herself to take such a drastic step? It had never been her intention for her plan to go so off the rails. It wasn't supposed to end with Wren losing her life. But she reflected on the information she had received from the sheriff and the ME, and realized how right she had been. Wren was willing to risk it all, even her own life, and the life of her unborn.

The pink bundle. The baby. Birdie never knew about the life growing inside Wren at the time of her disappearance and hadn't yet given thought to the realization that in all her visions, her sister held a pink blanket. Birdie wasn't ready to process the loss of another family member. Wren had deprived them all of the chance to treasure another life. Roy and Lula lost a grandchild. Iva and Marlow lost a sister. She lost another chance to get things right.

Wren sacrificed all of it for a text from a married man. Only the text had not come from the man with whom Wren hoped to make a new life. It came from Birdie herself.

The audacity of it all never needed to be known by another soul. Birdie wanted to believe that divulging her secret to her parents on their deathbed was an act of selfless grace. But she knew she would have taken it to her own grave if it weren't for her guilt. Roy and Lula left this world, knowing their responsible, reliable eldest daughter had taken a bold step to rid them all of their naivete and reveal to them what she had known since she was a child. She alone freed them all from the disappointment and upheaval that Wren doled out to them, all so shamelessly, without conscience. And she had done so with four simple words, whispered in their ears. The last words they heard before dying:

"I sent the text."

An anguished scream crept up from the bottom of her soul and was released—regret, sadness, and remorse resonated through the house. Hopelessness gripped her and threatened to keep her there, alone on the closet floor amid the clutter of her life. She wanted to lie down, bury her head in her hands, and cry until she fell asleep. She was so tired. But there was one thing left to do to make sure her secret was never revealed again.

She reached out with a shaky hand and grasped the

burner phone. It had been so simple. She asked one of her students to procure it for her. He needed a grade bump, and she was happy to oblige in exchange for the favor. He assured her it wouldn't be traceable and asked no questions about what she intended to do with the phone. She had even waited to send the text on the night of the storm. If Wren left in those conditions, her point could be driven home even more severely than she could have wished.

Over the years, she wondered what became of Wren that night. Her mind never landed on the idea that Wren might have been harmed by the text. She had convinced herself that her sister had reached out to the married man. Maybe he agreed to leave with her; maybe he had sent Wren away. Birdie didn't really care. She just knew Wren had jumped at the chance to run off with a married man, deserting her lifelong responsibilities without a second thought.

But now it was time to rid herself of this evidence. If she hoped to foster a better relationship with Iva and Marlow, the phone needed to disappear. After all, she told herself, she had ultimately done it for them. Right now, at this moment in their lives, they might not appreciate all that she had sacrificed, but someday they would. She was all the family they had now. Eventually, they would come around, she was sure of that.

Wren had caused them to lose so much. Birdie lost Jacob, lost the chance to become a mother, to live a life in which she was never alone. In a sense, Wren had robbed her of the things she wanted most in life. Then, adding salt to the wound, she disdainfully flaunted those gifts while she neglected them and took them for granted. She didn't deserve to be a mother. Wren got exactly what she was due. The baby was an unexpected consequence of her actions, one she would never forgive herself for.

Birdie left the mess on the closet floor. For now, her most ardent task was to make sure the phone was never found. She moved through the house, marveling at the quiet; grateful that she saw no sign of her sister, at least for now.

She got in her car and drove to Boomer Lake, one of the very places the real divide between her and her sister had become such an affliction for Birdie. The lake was quiet. A light, cold mist fell, so there were no late-night walkers getting in their required steps. Birdie parked near one of the boardwalks that stretched over the lake. She walked slowly, exhaustion winning over urgency. When she reached the end of the walkway, she made no grand gesture, simply let the phone slip from her grasp. Tiny bubbles rose to the water's surface as the old phone sunk to the bottom of the lake. Even if it were ever discovered, no one would know who had dumped it. Her secret was safe.

She was safe.

The drizzle turned to a heavier rain as she turned and slowly made her way back to her car. Once inside, she turned the car on and cranked the heater up as high as it would go, hoping it could remove the bone deep chill she felt. Just before she put the car in gear, she received a notification alert on her phone. She punched in the pass code and clicked the message icon.

UNKNOWN: ***It's not over yet, Birdie-Bird. Iva and Marlow need to know.***

Coming Soon

MUDDY WATER - SHADOWS OF CAMELOT CROSSING -
A HAUNTING IN STILLWATER, BOOK 3

Hours after Carly Bennett's father died, the recently deceased man settled into the old rocking chair in the corner of his oldest daughter's tiny bedroom.

Carly lie awake in her bed, wide-eyed, absorbing the news of her father's sudden passing. There were no tears, she felt no sadness.

A chill settled upon the room, and she rolled over, pulling the blankets up around her neck. She did not see her father as he silently watched her.

While she didn't notice his first visitation, Carly Bennett began seeing more of her father after he passed than she ever had while he was alive.

Acknowledgments

Thank you to my family for supporting me and my dream; my friends for cheering me on; and my amazing team of editors who helped make this happen for me … again! An extra shout out to Dar, Jordan and Zoe for tirelessly allowing me to question every minutiae, for reading those ugly first drafts and for always providing me with feedback, whether I wanted to hear it or not.

About the Author

Lisa Courtaway lives in Stillwater, Oklahoma and is married with four children. An entourage of six dogs follows her everywhere. She has worn many career-hats, from advertising to insurance to education. Currently she works as a media teaching assistant at an elementary school and is writing the third book in the Shadows of Camelot Crossing series.

She loves a good ghost story, and has lived in several homes that spoke to her in mysterious ways. True crime stories, watching a binge-worthy series, reading, and spending time with her family are her favorites.

Since she was young, people have often told her she should write a book ... so she did ... and then did it again ... and she plans to keep doing so.

You can find out more about Lisa, including her social media links, and content at her website:

www.lisacourtaway.com

Also By Lisa Courtaway

Red Water – Shadows of Camelot Crossing, A Haunting in
Stillwater, Book 1

Made in United States
Troutdale, OR
10/18/2023

13815977R00154